Slip and Fall
A Harry's Pottery Mystery

Holly Jacobs

Slip and Fall

Dedication: To John McCall, who knows stuff. A lot of stuff.

Dear Reader,

She's baaaack! Thank you everyone who picked up Harry's first book, *A View to a Kiln,* and asked for more! You'll notice a small shout out to my other cozy mystery series, *Maid in LA* in this new one. I love bringing older books into newer books. Quincy's one of my all-time bestsellers.

Fiction frequently has some foundation in fact. Harry's no exception. You see, I have my own pottery studio. But unlike Harry, I've never been the subject of a murder investigation... much less two. That's right, there's another murder connected to Harry's Pottery and Harry's got to figure out who-dunnit.

In case you missed it, *A View to a Kiln* was a Jeopardy answer! That's right. I didn't know that was a goal until it happened! You can check it out on my website...www.HollyJacobs.com.

I really hope you enjoy Harry's second book! As always, thank you so much for all your support.

Holly Jacobs

Harry's Pottery Mystery Series:
1. *A View to a Kiln*
2. *Slip and Fall*

Prologue

"She's dead," I said, trying the words on for size. "That's awful."

"She's dead and I'm here to take you down to the station," Micci said.

"Wait. What?" Come to the station. It almost sounded like...

"How did she die?" I asked slowly.

"She was murdered..."

Chapter One

Slip: A liquid clay that is about the consistency of heavy cream.
~Harry's Pottery

Eight Days Earlier

I looked out the window that separated my ceramic workspace from the sales floor and groaned.

The three ladies who had just come in were *gawkers*. I'd learned to recognize the type in the last few weeks.

It seems if you find a dead body in your kiln, your pottery studio gets a bit of a reputation and people wanted to check it out.

They come to gawk.

I originally separated my storefront and studio with a glass wall to keep the dust out of the store...but now I was glad because it gave me some cover.

Things had *died down*—I stopped myself. I planned to strike that particular phrase from my lexicon.

Things had *settled down* since I found that body a little less than a month ago. And then the news broke that someone had been arrested for putting that body in my kiln and *Harry's Pottery* was back in the paper. And with that came the gawkers.

I tried to ignore them as I worked on throwing a bowl off the hump. *Throwing off the hump* meant I took a big glob of clay and threw a number of smaller objects from it. In this case, I was throwing bowls.

I wet my hand and pulled the side of the bowl higher.

I saw one of the women point at me in my periphery vision and studiously kept my eye on bowl.

It was easier dealing with bowls than with random strangers' curiosity. And I resented it. I'd come home from Thanksgiving dinner and stayed up late decking the shop out for the holidays. I'd strung a ribbon across the front windows and filled it with small ceramic ornaments. I'd dated them and if they sold well, I'd do more next year and try to build off that.

If I could get people to make buying a *Harry's Pottery* ornament a Christmas tradition I'd have a guaranteed revenue stream.

Being a small business owner meant I had to do more than be creative, I had to think like a businesswoman. Even the shop's holiday decorations were part of marketing.

I looked out at my decked-out-for-the-holiday shop and felt another stab of guilt.

I knew I should get up and help Phyllis—my father's new fiancée—who was filling in at the register today. This wasn't her normal gig and she was here to help me out while my regular weekend help was out of town on an extended visit.

Yes, I knew I should go help her, but I was in no hurry to. I really felt as if I'd reached the end of my rope. I was done with gawkers and the new macabre reputation my small pottery store had garnered through no fault of its own.

No fault of my own.

I'd finish these pieces and hopefully the gawkers would be gone. I'd go out and check on Phyllis then, I promised myself. She was sweet to offer to come help. Especially so close to her wedding.

That's when I saw her. No, not Phyllis...Velma Harris.

Velma toddled her way into the storefront, swaying to and fro. She almost swayed into the ceramic Christmas town scene I'd painstakingly made and displayed in the shop's front window.

I threw a plastic bag on my hump—which didn't sound right even in my head—wiped my hand on a towel as I hurried through the door that separated my workspace from the shop.

I felt as if I were moving in slow motion.

I was aware of the gawkers tittering as I came out onto the sales floor in my clay splattered apron.

I saw Phyllis behind the register smile at me.

And I saw Velma tottering this way and that, her cane swaying in the air like a tightrope walker's pole, looking for some balance in thin air, just missing a shelf of mugs.

Just as I reached her, she toppled over, almost in slow motion. She grabbed onto that shelf and for on split second, I swear she smiled at me.

Velma was on the floor, along with that shelf full of mugs.

"Oh, Velma, are you okay?" I asked as I knelt down with my repeat, never-buy-anything, customer. Adi, my occasional assistant, always kept an eye out for her. But Adi was still with her family—not that I blamed her for getting away— and Phyllis couldn't have known about Velma.

Not that I knew anything for sure, but I suspected.

Velma had been coming in on occasion for months. Something just felt off about her. Adi and I started noting the dates of her visit the second time she came in. It felt like she was casing the store, although at her age, I couldn't imagine she planning to break in.

No, that second visit, she almost fell.

And the third.

And the fourth.

We made it a point to be close at hand whenever she entered the shop.

But I hadn't made it in time this visit.

"Oh, my neck," Velma cried. "You'd better call an ambulance."

"An ambulance?" I asked.

"I'm sure I did something. I can feel it. At my age, everything is fragile."

I wasn't sure what Velma's age was. Somewhere between sixty and a hundred. I truly

11

couldn't tell if she was on the older side of that range and had aged well, or if she was on the younger side and hadn't aged well at all.

"Hurry. Someone call 911," Velma cried.

Phyllis picked up the phone and made the call. The gawkers gawked, taking everything in.

"Your floor was wet and I slipped," Velma said.

My attorney-sense kicked in. Yes, before I was a humble potter, I was an attorney. I don't think there's such a thing as a truly humble attorney, though I'd done my best.

I might not be a working attorney any more, but I couldn't totally eradicate what I knew. And I knew that Velma was out for something.

"There's not water on the floor," I said simply. And without another thought, I pulled my cellphone from my pocket and took a few pictures of the scene, from the door, to the Velma's feet and the obvious lack of any moisture under them.

Her eyes narrowed.

I took a picture of her face as well. A close up.

"Maybe it was all the dust from all the clay you use," she said slowly. "It's very dusty."

I smiled and took a few more pictures of the shelves near Velma. They were dust free. "No, ma'am, I can't imagine that's it. I installed the glass between where I work and where customers come on purpose. We try to keep a spotless and dustless shop.

Her lips pursed, joining her narrowed eyes. "Well, I fell on something."

"Maybe it's just your age," I said as sweetly as I could, though I laced it with all the snarkiness I could manage. "I know that many old people have problems with balance."

Velma couldn't mask her raw anger at that comment.

If I was wrong about her, that crack was probably one of the meanest things I'd ever said. But I didn't think I was wrong.

"The ambulance is on the way," Phyllis said.

"Phyllis could you get the other customers' names and contact info? Just in case we need them. And please, ladies, pick a mug—an unbroken mug—as an apology for interrupting your shopping. I hope you come back again soon."

Phyllis started to talk to the gawkers and Velma moaned.

"You'd better contact your insurance company," Velma said softly between the moans.

"Because?" I asked.

"I fell on your property," she said, again with that hint of an almost-smile.

"I see," was all I said. I snapped another picture of her face, capturing that almost-smile.

"Yes. I suspect it's going to take me a long while to heal." She moaned again. "I've heard that making insurance claims can really impact your payments. We could probably find a way to keep this between you and me," she said slowly, watching me as she made the offer.

She moaned again.

"I see," I said again. I paused, studying her closely. "Velma, do you know what I used to do before I opened Harry's Pottery?"

She stopped moaning and said, "No."

"I was an attorney. I worked with all kinds of people. I've become quite the judge of character."

"An attorney?" she asked slowly, drawing those four syllables into the length a dozen syllables might take.

I didn't say anything. I just continued to stare at her.

"And you think your attorney-spidey senses gives you some insight about me?" she asked.

I smiled. I got up and blatantly took more pictures of the shop, of the area around Velma, and of Velma herself.

Velma's eyes narrowed until they were barely slits and she glared at me.

I got a picture of that, too.

I didn't need to say anything else, as the ambulance had arrived. "Velma, would you like me to come with you, or can I call someone for you?" I asked sweetly.

The gawkers smiled at my concern, but Velma glared. "No. I'm sure the ambulance crew will get me to the hospital just fine."

I grabbed a card from the counter. "Please give us a call and let us know how you are," I said. "We'll all be very worried about you. I mean, women your age who falls for no reason...there might be some serious underlying medical condition or something else dire going on. So please keep us posted."

Velma glared. "You can be sure you'll hear from me."

I suspected I would.

And I suspected this wasn't the first time Velma had pulled this kind of scam.

Yes, I was sure it was a scam. I couldn't prove it in a court of law at the moment, but I didn't think this was her first slip and fall claim. Adi and I had suspected she was up to something. Now I knew what.

After the EMTs took Velma away on a stretcher, Phyllis said, "Oh, Harry, you've had quite a time of it lately."

"Yes. Yes I have." I tried not to sound too whiny, but I suspect I did.

I just wanted my normal, quiet life back, but it seemed the universe had other ideas.

I tried to keep Velma out of my thoughts as I went back to work. But she kept inserting herself in between my thoughts on pottery. I just couldn't seem to help myself.

Adi and I had saved her from other almost-falls. I checked our book. Five visits since June.

To be honest, we watched her like a hawk when she came in. Either she was having major balance issues, or she was looking to make a buck off my business's insurance.

15

After her comment, I changed that thought to make a buck without going through insurance, which made sense. It would leave less of a trail if I paid her in cash. And if you were a scam artist, a paper trail was the last thing you wanted.

I was pretty sure I was right, but time would tell.

There was nothing I could do about it now.

I went back to work on the wheel, but knew my heart wasn't in it.

Normally, I was a very strict taskmaster. I treated my job at the studio like I'd treated my job when I'd reported to an office every day. I buckled down and got my work done.

There was no room for not-feeling-like it.

Work was work.

But given the last month, even I couldn't be too hard on myself.

I took off my studio apron, which was a mess. I cleaned up a bit and went out to the shop to help poor Phyllis, who'd proclaimed working a register on black Friday was fun.

My father was about to marry a very nice woman.

In between customers, I asked her about the wedding. They weren't wasting time. They'd asked me to save the date...the weekend before Christmas.

Dad joked it was for tax purposes, but anyone looking at the two of them together knew it was more than that.

"I want something simple," Phyllis said. "We talked to Judge Mike and he said he'd come officiate. Just our family and a few close friends at the house. Champagne and cake afterward. Easy peasy, lemon squeezy."

How could you not love a woman who used a phrase *easy-peasy-lemon-squeezy*?

"Harry," she said softly, "the thing that matters most to me is your father. I don't need fuss or frou-frou things. I just need him."

I felt very lucky that this woman was about to marry my dad. Very lucky that she was about to be my stepmother. "I'm so glad he found you."

She laughed. "He didn't," she said. "I found him and recognized a good thing when I saw it."

I was sure there was a lot of truth in that statement. My father was an expert when it came to the law, but when it came to people? His social skills were lacking. It had taken him until just last month to let me know he respected my decision to give up the law and follow my passion...pottery.

Maybe Phyllis was a good influence.

She certainly had no trouble showing her feelings.

The rest of the day went quickly. There was hardly a moment to catch my breath. I sold a lot of the inventory on display and had to reload the shelves more than once.

As a small business owner, I knew that Black Friday and the holiday season were my best income producing streams. I'd spent most of the year preparing for it. I'd amassed a healthy inventory to draw from...even with the stock Velma had broken.

At five, I flipped the sign from *Open* to *Closed*.

I'd thought about extending my hours on Black Friday, but opted not to. I'd reopen in the morning, and people were welcome to come back then.

"Wow," I said.

"Wow is right," Phyllis repeated. "That was crazy."

"A good crazy," I said. "I can afford to keep the lights on a bit longer."

"Are you doing okay?" Phyllis asked, looking concerned.

"Sorry, just my weird sense of humor. I am doing fine for a new business. I'm lucky. I can always pick up some contract work if money's tight. Dad's been great about that."

Maybe I should have seen that as his attempt to support my dream. But I hadn't. I felt bad about that now. It was too easy to guess at someone's motives and shape them to suit your own view of a story.

My father had encouraged me to go to law school and dissuaded me from being an art major. All these years later it had been easy to see that incident as a way to think he didn't approve of my leaving the law and opening my studio.

I'd been wrong.

I would be more careful about making those kinds of assumptions in the future. If I'd just come out and asked, I could have saved us both a lot of grief.

I smiled again at my almost-stepmom and tried to reassure her about my income. "I'll still have my classes the first week of December, but then they're canceled until the new year. I'm starting a new class then, which was a nice steady source of income. All in all, it was a great year."

A great year except for the dead body in my kiln, I thought but didn't say.

I didn't plan on mentioning the dead-body-kiln ever again if I could help it. *The Kiln Killer* had been found. That was enough. I was not going to mention or even think about the unfortunate incident again.

The dead body had turned out to be a less than nice man. I felt bad for thinking that particular thought, but somehow it made things easier knowing he'd been the master of his own demise.

"What about your accident victim?" Phyllis asked.

"I was going to call the hospital and see if she was admitted, so I can check on her." I thought she was scamming me, but it made sense to check.

"That's a great idea. I'm going to head to your father's for dinner. He said he'd cook. And by cook he meant reheat Thanksgiving leftovers. Would you like to come for dinner?" she asked.

"No, but thanks. Micah said he was coming over and cooking for me."

It was hard to believe I'd really only known Micah McCain for a month. There'd been an immediate spark, but when you're recovering from a divorce, finding a body in your kiln, and aren't sure if a guy's available...you take things slow.

Turns out I was totally recovered from my divorce, I solved the body in my kiln mystery and Micah was absolutely, totally available.

Now that things had quieted down, maybe it was time to rethink our relationship speed.

Phyllis smiled. "Micah's one of my favorite's at the law firm...well, other than your father."

Phyllis had gone to work for my father. That's how they'd met. So of course she knew Micah. "He's a gentleman," she said. "He always asks the support staff for help. He doesn't bark orders like some attorneys."

I didn't know how he acted at work, but I knew how he'd treated me. I concurred, "Yes, gentleman is just the word for Micah."

I told Micah as much an hour later as he was making scallops in my small kitchen in the apartment above the shop.

I'd gone all out decking the halls in the shop, but I hadn't done any decorating up here yet. Closer to Christmas I'd get a tree...a live tree. I had a box of ornaments I'd made over the years.

And nine ornaments from my mother. She'd bought me one every year from a Baby's First Christmas to the Christmas Angel she'd bought before she died.

That angel was always the eye-level front of the tree ornament.

It's the one that meant the most to me.

I'd put all those ornaments up along with small LED lights, then I'd string popcorn.

And maybe, if I were lucky, Micah would help.

The thought made me smile and so did his grousing.

He groaned. *"Gentleman* is a not a compliment."

"Gentleman is a huge compliment," I assured him.

"Agree to disagree. Gentleman is the word your Bubbi uses to describe the guy she wants to set you up with. Real men prefer descriptions like..." He was obviously stuck on a real-man description.

"Stud?" I offered.

He nodded. "It's better than *gentleman.* It's better than saying he has a sense of humor, too. Yeah, that's not a real recommendation either." He sighed and pushed his glasses higher on his nose. They seemed to amplify the color of his eyes. Some people might say they were blue.

But his eyes needed more description than that.

Ice blue. That's how I'd describe them. And his glasses only seemed to amplify the color.

21

Or maybe amplify the iciness. Or maybe it was that he had such a dark complexion and dark hair. His eyes seemed out of place.

No matter what it was, his eyes were one of his best features, and that was saying a lot because all his features were good.

I'd always wished for dark, flowing locks. Instead I had frizzy, red Medusa hair.

I sighed.

So did he and mumbled the word *gentleman* again, which made me laugh.

I think that was his intent because he smiled and asked, "So how was the rest of the day, it being Black Friday and all?"

"I got everything decorated before I opened the doors and that's a good start. Phyllis was amazing. I'll have to go over the books, but I can say unequivocally that the sales were better than I thought they'd be. That's good news."

"It is. Let's toast to better sales." He raised his wine glass.

I raised my glass of white wine as well. He toasted as he flipped a scallop.

We air clinked and he flipped another scallop as he took a sip. He was a man of many skills.

"But good news isn't the only news," I said. "Velma finally fell."

"Velma?" he asked.

"She's been visiting the studio for a few months. I looked it up. This was her fifth visit. Five times since June. And she'd never bought anything. She stopped coming in after the unfortunate kiln incident, but she came back today."

"And?" Micah prompted.

"Like I said, she finally fell. Adi and I had a feeling she was going to try something. I mean, who goes shopping at a store that many times and never buys anything? I suspect I'll get a call in a few days." I'd added my own contemporaneous notes to our notebook after Velma was gone. Between those and the pictures, I'd done everything I could to shelter myself and my business, *Harry's Pottery*.

"Really? You think she's a scam artist?" Micah asked.

"I do. We documented all her visits and all her almost-falls. She came in four times before today and never bought a thing. We made it a habit of walking right next to her when she came in. Every time she tripped or wobbled, one of us caught her. But Adi wasn't here and Phyllis didn't know. I tried to get out there when I saw her, but it was too late."

"Did you call the ambulance?" he asked.

"Yes, I did. She asked me to because I think she wanted to intimidate me, but I wanted to be sure to have her *injuries*," I air-quoted the word, "or lack thereof were documented."

"Good idea," he said.

"I did some research after her first few almost-falls. I didn't find anything online or in the news about her, but I suspect she settles each case. She made mention of keeping it from the insurance company today. She'd want to keep her name out of the paper or official court documents. Some nice, quiet pay-off would be more her style."

"So what are you going to do?" he asked.

"I called the hospital, and of course, they couldn't tell me anything." I took another sip of wine.

"HIPAA," Micah said.

I nodded. "Right. They're all about privacy. But then I called the front desk to ask for her room, and there was no one admitted by that name. I'll try again tomorrow, but I suspect she got sent home."

"That should help your case," he said.

"It should," I said.

"I take it you won't willingly accept an insurance or private settlement?"

"No. I may not work as an attorney, but I'm still committed to justice." I laughed. "That sounded so sanctimonious. Truth, justice, and the American way and all that. But it's the truth."

I suspected I was not Velma's first mark, but I didn't intend to become her victim. "My insurance might willingly make a settlement, but I won't. I'll fight her claims in court. I suspect having her name bandied about in the paper—and I'll do what I can to get coverage—will annoy her. It will make future scams harder for her, at least here in Erie."

Micah served me a plate of pasta with a light garlic sauce and the scallops, and thinly sliced fresh basil on top, then took the seat next to me with his own plate.

He leaned over and kissed my cheek. "You're cute when you get fired up."

"Was that a ceramic pun?" I asked.

He looked confused and I realized it wasn't. "*Kiln. Firing a kiln. Fired up.* Angry," I prompted.

Micah laughed. "No, I'm not that good."

Even if he hadn't intended the quip, I laughed. That was what I liked about spending time with Micah...when he wasn't infuriating me, he made me laugh.

I took a bite of dinner and said, "You are more than good enough."

Lily, my dog, came into the room and sat next to Micah. She delicately placed her large wolfhound head on his lap. And sure enough, he broke a piece of Italian bread off and fed it to her.

"You are a gentleman, a heck of a cook, and a very soft touch," I informed him.

"Spurious lies," he said, laughing.

Being with Micah was easy. I liked it.

And I suspected I was coming to rely on it.

He'd been my lawyer for the unfortunate incident. Now, he was just my...*boyfriend.* I hadn't said the word out loud yet. He hadn't said girlfriend either, as far as I knew. But we spent most of our free time together. At first because of the unfortunate incident, but now because we wanted to.

Even as he was preparing for a big case, he found time to be with me.

I hadn't wanted to ask him what we were because I hadn't wanted to name it, but the thought didn't scare me any longer.

The truth of the matter was that Micah was my boyfriend.

I was his girlfriend.

After my marriage fell apart, I decided to concentrate on getting my business off the ground. It was easy not to think about a new relationship when it was all I could do to keep up with the shop, making pottery and working for my dad when time allowed and my income required.

But now I thought about a relationship.

Specifically, a relationship with Micah McCain.

And I liked the thought.

Chapter Two

"Turning an avocation into a vocation takes a lot of planning. Especially when the avocation involves art. There's a reason why the term 'Starving Artist' became a thing.
~Harry's Pottery

The following Monday, I hung up the phone, stuck it in my pocket and stood there, feeling a bit shell-shocked.

"Harry, are you okay?" Adi asked. She was back from her extended visit to her family in Philadelphia. She'd come in today while the shop was closed—we were closed on Sundays and Mondays—to visit.

We both needed to talk about what had happened last month.

I was pretty sure our friendship was going to be all right. And Adi had said she definitely wanted to keep working for me, especially now that she was single-parenting again.

Her four-year-old daughter, Nori, was happily playing with clay in the studio as we talked things out.

When the store's phone had rung, Adi had picked it up out of instinct. She'd handed it over to me and in under ten minutes, I had a conference call scheduled for the following day.

"So what was that about?" Adi asked again as I hung up

"I've always liked Mondays, but I think I'm going to like them a whole lot more after this." I tried to digest what the woman on the other end of the line had just said. "It was an editor. She read about me and *Harry's Pottery* in the paper...she's from Erie and gets the paper online. She checked out the store's site and read some of my blog posts there. They want me to write a book."

"Pardon?" Adi said.

I nodded. "I know. *Pardon*? I think I said that every other word. She said she'd call back tomorrow. Paula. Paula Stone. She wants to talk about me writing a book on pottery, switching careers, and small businesses and..." I shrugged. "She loved my pieces on our website and said that she had a lot of writers who used to be attorneys. When she read about what happened here and my background, she thought I might have something to say in a book."

"*Harry's Pottery: A How-to Live Your Dream and Start a Small Business.* I like it," Adi said.

I shook my head. "I'm not sure. It feels like I'm capitalizing on a tragedy."

"I've seen your notebook," Adi said. "You scribble in it all the time."

"I'm mainly making notes to myself about a different project. How I glazed a piece. The process of making it." It was a handy way to keep track of what worked and what didn't.

"And…?" she prompted.

"Maybe I add little tidbits now and then." Those tidbits frequently became my website's blog posts. I didn't do them too often, but there were enough to keep someone interested reading for a while.

Some of them might be used as a footprint for the book. I realized I was already mentally figuring out how an entire book would work.

"You have the stuff on the website," Adi said as if she could read my mind, "and your business notebook." She grinned. "I think all those tidbits are what's going to interest Paula Stone. I'd pull out a few for your talk tomorrow. What time is she calling?"

"Noon.," I said.

"Great," Adi said, as if noon was the best time in the entire world. "I'll get here about eleven thirty to man the front store while you talk."

"You're not scheduled—" I started to protest.

Adi interrupted. "I'll be here."

At that moment, someone rang my doorbell. A little alert showed up on my cellphone. I clicked it and saw Barnabas waving at the camera.

"Guess who's here," I said as I moved toward the door. I couldn't help grinning as I opened it and my neighbor walked in. He was a big man who seemed to fill every room he entered. Not because of his bigness, but because of the size of his heart. That heart was his most prominent feature. Some people would say his dark brown eyes or his bald head. Maybe some would mention complexion, which reminded me of my favorite clay that had been well-fired.

Okay, I'm not sure he'd appreciate his complexion being compared to clay, but it made sense to me.

All those things were things strangers noticed. Once you met him, it was definitely his heart that stood out.

"Barnabas," Nori screamed as she got up from the workbench and launched herself at him, clay-hands and all.

Lily, the laziest dog in the universe, got up off her studio dog bed and raced over to him as well, yapping happily.

I looked at Adi and saw her shy smile.

I knew Barnabas liked Adi and I was pretty sure she liked him back. The chaos in the shop over the last month had brought them closer...that was a good thing in my humble opinion.

"I just thought I'd stop and see if anyone's interested in some dinner. Mama Lonnie sent over enough lasagna to feed an army," he said merrily.

Barnabas was one of my favorite people in the world, and not just because his mother was an amazing cook. But having Mama Lonnie around cooking was definitely a bonus. It would be interesting to see her and Micah in a cook-off. I'd be happy to act as judge, even though I was sure I'd have to proclaim it a tie. They both were that good.

"What about you, Lady Bug?" he asked me.

But with thoughts of tomorrow's call, I found myself shaking my head. "I'd love to, but I have a business call tomorrow and need to get some material ready for it. But I bet you can convince Adi and Nori."

"Adi? You wouldn't make me eat that lasagna all by myself, would you?" Barnabas asked.

"Yes. We'd be delighted to help you out." She turned to me, a huge smile on her face. "I'll see you tomorrow."

"Thanks," I said.

I watched as the two bundled up Nori and left.

They made quite a pair.

Adi claimed she was five five, but that's only because she never was without heels. Even in the snow. She was tiny, with dark hair, a super fair complexion, even in the summer, and a ready smile. Barnabas towered over Adi. And yet...

Barnabas and Adi each held one of Nori's hands as they walked down the block toward his house. Barnabas had two clay dust handprints on his back.

I smiled at the sight.

They fit.

I thought Adi and Barnabas were meant for each other. I wasn't prone to matchmaking, but in this case, I might make an exception.

Maybe I could—

My cellphone rang, interrupting the thought.

I locked the door as I picked up as I pulled it out and saw Micah's name.

I smiled as I answered.

"Hey, are you still coming over?" I asked, anxious to see him.

Witnessing Barnabas and Adi's blossoming relationship reminded me of my own connection to Micah and it reminded me that I missed him. I couldn't wait to tell him about the call.

"Sorry. I'm working late tonight," he said.

I was disappointed, but I didn't want Micah to know that. "No problem," I said as nonchalantly as I could manage. "I understand how that goes."

"I just called to say I miss you." His voice was a bit gritty. That low burr in it made me go all warm and gooey inside.

"I miss you, too. But I'll see you tomorrow?" I half asked and half offered.

"Yes. See you then," he promised as he hung up.

I was still holding my phone when an unknown number called on the store phone. I almost let it go to voicemail, but found myself picking it up. "Harry's Pottery. Can I help you?"

"This is Shawn Hawkins, Esquire. That's S. H. A. W. N I'm the attorney for Velma Harris..."

I picked up a pen and took notes as S.H.A.W.N. Esquire talked. I listened as he explained Velma had suffered long-term damage from her fall and they were holding *Harry's Pottery* responsible.

All I could think of was Micah had just finished representing me and now he was going to be back on the clock.

I wasn't overly concerned about the suit.

Annoyed? Yes.

But I felt my documentation was going to provide a layer of protection.

When Shawn said we could discuss settling out of court and without bothering the insurance company, I felt even more convinced I was right.

Velma had done this before.

I asked for his contact information. He said he'd call again tomorrow and hung up before I could insist.

I thought about calling Micah right away, but held off. If he was working late, he was in the thick of something and I didn't want to interrupt his work.

Luckily, there was leftover pasta from the night before. I fed Lily, nuked a bowl, and opened up my laptop. I started searching Velma's name. I went to our local paper's site and tried her name. Velma Harris. Nothing. I did a basic Google search. Still nothing.

On a hunch, I ran a search on her attorney. Shawn Hawkins. I tried Hawkens. Hockens. Huckens.

Weird.

I ran a search on my father.

His name popped up under his law firm, but also different articles that had been written about his clients and their trials.

I went to the Pennsylvania Bar's website and plugged in Shawn's name. Every way I could think to spell it in every combination I could think of. Still nothing.

I couldn't help but smile.

I was pretty sure both Velma and her "attorney" were scam artists.

I couldn't wait for the next call from Shawn, Esquire.

Feeling as if I'd done everything I could do until Velma and Shawn made their next move, I pulled out one of my notebooks and started to make notes for the editor. If I were to write a book, I wouldn't really want a pottery how-to. As much as I loved what I did, I hadn't done it long enough to feel confident in trying to tell someone else how to do pottery.

But I did feel confident enough to talk about switching careers. Following your passion. Setting up a new business. Of course, there would be some clay talk, but that wouldn't be the focus.

I jotted a few pages of notes. I was ready for Paula's call the following day. Then I let Lily out and we both went to bed.

I'd only just turned off the light when my cellphone rang.

I smiled when I saw Micah's name.

"Hey, what's up?" I asked.

"I just called to say goodnight," he said.

"Goodnight. How did work go?" I asked.

"I think I'm ready. How was your night?"

"I did some research. I've got lots to tell you, but it'll wait until tomorrow."

"Just promise me you weren't investigating another murder." He added a laugh at the end of the sentence, but it didn't quite cover up his concern.

"No murders," I promised. "I'm done with that. I was researching a small, slip and fall case and working on ideas for a book."

"Do tell about both," he said.

"Tomorrow," I promised. "I've got to get some sleep. I have a call with an editor tomorrow."

He laughed. "Way to keep me in suspense."

"Maybe I just want to give you a reason to come see me tomorrow," I said.

"Harry, I don't need any other reason other than the fact I miss you. Night."

We hung up and as I snuggle next to Lily, I smiled at the thought of seeing Micah the next day.

The next morning, I had a cup of coffee in one hand and my notebook in the other as I tried to get ready for that phone interview with the editor.

I wasn't sure if I wanted to write a book.

Oh, I did love writing. More than that, I loved research. I think that's why I finally followed my father's plan for me and became a lawyer... I really loved the research. I loved taking random bits of information, finding a common thread and pulling them all together.

And yet writing would take me away from my pottery.

And I quit being a lawyer in order to pursue my art.

And I wouldn't mind doing the research and writing.

And it might prove to be a nice little boost to my hit-or-miss income stream.

Round and round.

Round and round.

My thoughts chased after each other in a rather circular manner.

Adi and Nori arrived at eleven.

"You're early," I said with a smile.

"I wanted to give you time to get ready if you needed more time. And with all the customers lately, I figured you could use the help."

Nori had gone to the table behind the register and announced, "I'm gonna make Barnabas a picture 'cause he made me dinner and you gotta say thank you when someone does something nice for ya."

Adi shot Nori a look so full of love and pride it turned me all mushy.

"She's amazing," I said as Nori settled down to work on her thank you card.

"She is," Adi agreed. "I worried that after everything that went on she'd be upset, but her dad has never been around much, so not seeing him hasn't really impacted her. I told her he has to go away for a while, and she seemed to accept it."

"She'll be fine," I said. And I silently promised to do what I could to help Adi with Nori.

"I hope so," Adi said, staring at her daughter with such naked love it was palpable.

"So how was dinner?" I asked.

"Great," was all she said.

I thought I saw a distinct pinkening of her cheeks. "You can't just leave it at that," I prompted.

"There's not much to tell. We went over to Barnabas's, had dinner. Nori played with the two dogs Barnabas brought home. We couldn't stay too long because I didn't want to leave Miss Muffet to her own devices too long."

"If you'd known you were going to dinner, she could have come and hung out with me and Lily." The offer was sincere, but truly, Nori's dog Miss Muffet was a handful. Lily had adapted to live as a studio dog as if she'd been born to it.

Miss Muffet was definitely not born to it.

The few times she'd visited the shop, she'd wreaked havoc.

Adi saw the offer for what it was—the act of a true friend.

She laughed. "I appreciate it, but she's settling in nicely at home. I want to keep her to her routine."

"Well, if you need her to visit, Lily and I will always make it work. And we can always walk over and let her out if you need us too."

Adi lived less than a mile from the shop.

That was one of the nice things about Erie. It was the fourth biggest city in Pennsylvania, but it was at heart, a small town.

It was rare to go shopping and not bump into someone I knew.

Even driving from one side of the city to the other was quick. Under a half hour. Which in a big city was nothing.

Here in Erie we complained about how far it was to go from the east-side to the west-side.

My house and studio were pretty much center city, right along the bayfront. I felt that made me impartial, but the rest of Erie tended to stack up decidedly east or decidedly west.

"Why don't you go in the back and get ready for your call. I'll handle things out here," Adi said.

"Thanks," I said.

I went over my notes and was ready when Paula called.

Talking to Paula helped calm me down a bit. She laid out what she envisioned. I told her about the notes I'd already made. She said if I could turn those notes into a solid proposal, she was pretty sure she could get me a nice little advance.

When I went back out to the shop, Adi was just finishing up with a customer.

"So how'd it go?" she asked.

"Good. I need to write up a proposal, three sample chapters, and then send it to her."

Adi grinned. "That's great."

"Mama, can we take my card to Mr. Barnabas's?" Nori asked, holding up her masterpiece.

"I think we could drop it off before we head home." Adi again had that faint pink tinge to her cheeks.

"When are you seeing Barnabas again?" I asked.

She sighed. "He asked about this weekend, but I didn't give him an answer. I said I'd check."

"Do you want to see him?" I didn't really need to ask because I knew the answer. Anyone who'd seen Adi with Barnabas knew the answer.

"Yes, but Harry, you more than most know that my life's a mess right now. Barnabas is a good man. He doesn't deserve to dive into the chaos that is my life."

"Can I be honest?" I asked.

She nodded. "Always."

"I think Barnabas would happily jump into any mess or chaos for you." I didn't feel the least bit presumptuous making that statement. I'd seen the looks that Barnabas had given Adi. I wouldn't define it for him, but I suspected I knew the depths of his feelings and I knew he'd do anything for her.

"Maybe I'll call him," she finally said.

I nodded as if her statement was no big deal...but I knew that it was.

I wanted nothing more for my friends than to be happy, and more and more I was beginning to suspect their path to happiness led to each other

After Adi and Nori left, I spent the rest of the afternoon making Post-Its for a potential *Harry's Pottery* book. I put them on my Idea Board.

It was nice to see something other than murder suspects on it.

I was taking the Idea Board back to its roots. *Ideas.*

Ideas were much better than suspects.

My business phone rang. I normally let it go to voicemail after hours, but a handset was sitting next to the Idea Board. I reached over and picked it up without thinking. "Hello. Harry's Pottery."

"I'd like to speak to the owner," a male voice said. I was pretty sure it was Shawn.

"This is she."

"It's Shawn Hawkins, Esquire again and I was hoping to speak to you about a settlement for my client, Velma Harris."

Uh oh. I grabbed a piece of paper and pen, ready to transcribe the conversation.

"Yes?" I said as noncommittally as I could.

"We think it would be advantageous for everyone involved to solve this quickly and quietly. Mrs. Harris, a devoted customer, suffered significant injuries after her fall at your business."

"Yes?" Monosyllabic. That's what I was going for.

"We thought a cash settlement between you and my client would help her pay for her medical bills as well as her pain and suffering, and by not involving your insurance company, you don't run the risk of increased premiums. Like I mentioned the other day, by keeping it quiet, you don't run the risk of more bad press for your little shop."

"More bad press?" I asked.

"Finding a body in your shop can't be good for business," he said.

I didn't feel inclined to mention that it had been very good for business in a rather macabre way. I wasn't going to say more than absolutely necessary to this man.

He named a cash amount that left me choking on nothing but air. I wanted to tell him that this was a new, small business and I didn't have access to that kind of cash. I wanted to tell him to shove his offer up his...

I took a deep breath and my best lawerly voice said, "Mr. Hawkins, please put your offer in writing and send it to me care of the shop. I'll have my attorney go over it and get back to you."

"Get back to me soon," he warned. "This generous offer won't last for long."

I didn't mention the documentation of Velma's visits. I didn't mention the pictures I'd taken. I didn't mention the fact that I was questioning this man's credentials. I just said, "Thank you for your call."

"Aren't you going to ask about my client's wellbeing?" he asked before I could hang up.

I didn't want to just ignore the question and give him ammunition against me, citing my callousness. But I didn't want to say more than I had to. "My attorney has advised me against speaking with you. If you want to share information, that would be wonderful, but I am not permitted to ask questions or offer information."

Plus he'd said she'd received significant injuries.

"She's in a great deal of pain," he said, maybe hoping to evoke some comment of sympathy, that he could use against me.

"Thank you for the information and for your call, Mr. Hawkins."

I hung up.

Moments later, there was a knock on the front door. I glanced through the window that separated my studio from the sales floor and saw Micah at the door. He gave me a small wave.

Some of my frustration evaporated. More than some.

I all but forgot it as I waved back and hurried to let him in.

"How was your day?" I asked as he came in.

He leaned down and kissed me. "Better now."

"Me, too."

"So catch me up on your cryptic comment last night," he said.

I did. I started with the book.

"I talked to the editor. I think it went well. I started putting up some ideas on what a book might look like."

Then I filled him in on Velma.

"Harry, life with you will never be boring, will it?" It might have sounded like a question, but it was a statement.

"I'm not paying off a scam artist," I said.

"No, you're not," he agreed. "I'll help."

He glanced at my idea wall. "I'll confess, I prefer ideas to suspects."

"I was just thinking the same thing," I said.

Maybe a few years down the pike, we would say something like that and smile, but I wasn't there yet. I still woke up from horrible nightmares. Nightmares in which I discovered the body in my kiln again. Only in my dreams, he had glowing eyes and in some versions he even spoke to me.

A couple nights, ago the skeleton had asked me to dance.

I gave a small shudder over the memory.

"Yes, ideas are much better," I reiterated.

We went upstairs to my apartment, Lily in tow.

In the middle of dinner—Micah cooked, which was always preferable—as we talked about our days, I filled him in Shawn Hawkins, Esquire. "I tried to look him up, but I couldn't

43

find anything," I said. "I figure when he sends me the papers, I'll have a better idea who I'm dealing with."

"And—"

I interrupted what I suspected might be a Micah warning. "And before you lecture me, I'll admit that I know lawyers who represent themselves have fools for clients." I laughed. "I was very noncommittal and told him to put it in writing and send it to the shop. I took notes of the conversations as well."

"Good. If it comes to that, I'll represent you," he offered without my having to ask. This was getting to be a regular thing.

I nodded, accepting his offer. "You know, some people might think I'm dating you in order to get free legal representation."

"Would they be right?" he asked.

I shook my head. "Nah. I'm dating you for your..."

"Body? Intelligence? Wit? Charm?" he supplied.

I forked up a bite of pork chops and said, "Cooking."

"It's good to have something to offer a relationship." He grinned.

Relationship. It fit with the words boyfriend and girlfriend. I was going to need to add all three words to my vocabulary. What we had was new. It started under odd circumstances. But it was growing.

Micah agreed to take things slow, and I appreciated that. I did the mental calculations. Thursday would be a full month.

And that didn't seem that long when it came to dating someone, but during that month, I'd seen Micah almost every day. Days that I didn't see him we talked. I felt as if I knew him better than I'd ever known my ex, but I realized that all that knowing didn't make up for years of gathering stories.

I decided to put forth more effort in finding out more about him. I'd start this weekend. "Thursday's our anniversary," I said. "One full month. Let's celebrate this weekend. I'll take you out to dinner after the shop closes on Saturday."

"I'd like that," he said. "I know there are items you buy for gifts for certain anniversaries. Is there one for one month?"

"I think dinner together sounds just about right."

And I had an idea what I'd like to do after dinner.

With my *boyfriend*.

As his *girlfriend*.

In this new *relationship*.

But I wasn't planning to mention it now.

I did know that I'd definitely shave my legs before our date.

Chapter Three

"Whenever I break a pot, I automatically start singing or humming **Another One Bites the Dust.** *It can be very embarrassing if I find I'm signing out loud and there are people around."*
~Harry's Pottery

I was on pins and needles on Saturday as I waited on customers and watched the clock.

I'd made reservations at *The Sandpiper Inn* and had let Adi go wild in my closet. She'd picked out my dress for the evening.

After dinner, we'd head to *Down by the Bay*, where we'd had our first date. Well, we'd gone out because of my unfortunate incident, but I was going to count that post-dead-body meeting as our first date.

My friend Trisha worked at *Down by the Bay*.

Well, my new friend.

We'd met because she used to own this house and I'd wanted to know if she was involved with the body in my kiln, so maybe friend was too generous a description. Potential friend? Friendly acquaintance?

She'd shown her boss the sample mugs I'd made for the bar. He'd placed an order for thirty and said if they went over well, he'd order more.

I just had two more customers to take care of, then I was closing shop and starting to get ready for my date.

Oh, I'd have a couple hours, but I wanted tonight to be perfect.

The two ladies in question bought a couple plates. "Thank you for coming to *Harry's Pottery*. I hope we see you again soon."

"We've heard all the talk about your store and we weren't sure what to expect, but this was better than we imagined," said the darker haired lady.

"You have beautiful pieces," said the other one. "I'll be sure to tell my friends."

"Take a few cards. If your friends come in and mention your name, I'll make a note and you'll get ten percent off on your next visit," I offered. And thus a new promotion was born. I'd leave a note for Adi.

"Oh, that's lovely," said the dark-haired lady.

They each snatched a few cards and hollered, "Happy Holidays," as they walked to the door.

I followed them and said, "To you, too."

They chattered as they walked off my porch and onto the sidewalk. We had a sprinkling of snow. Nothing major yet. That made me nervous. Mother Nature might be trying to lull us into a false sense of security.

I went back inside, locked up and tidied up the showroom before I headed upstairs. I primed and pampered myself before I got dressed for the date.

Not a date. And really not even the date.

THE DATE. All caps.

I put on some makeup and imagined how the night would go. Me. Micah. A romantic dinner. Drinks at *our* bar, then home to...

My phone beeped, letting me know someone was at the door. I looked on the app and saw it was Detective Micci Dana. "Be right down," I said into the speaker. "Come over to the apartment door."

I was not wearing this dress in the studio. It deserved better than all that clay dust.

Like Trisha, I'd met Micci because of the unfortunate incident. She'd been the investigator of the case.

Now that the case was over, she was another potential friend. She was going to start pottery classes after the holidays.

"Hi, Mic. Come on in. I don't have long, but come on up. It's been an absolute crazy day. Wait until you hear—"

Micci's dark hair was in a ponytail and she wore the leather jacket she'd worn the first time I met her. She shook her head, sending her ponytail flipping, and cut me off. "Harry, this isn't a social call. I'm here to inform you that Velma Harris is dead."

"She's dead?" I parroted.

She'd been old. Or at least older, but still she'd seemed fine when she'd been in.

I felt a stab of guilt.

I'd suspected Velma of fraud. I thought she fell on purpose to try to coerce money out of me and my insurance company. And now the poor woman was dead. "She's dead," I said, trying the words on for size. "That's awful."

"She's dead and I'm here to take you down to the station," Micci said.

That stopped me. I felt a bit muddled as I tried to work out what Micci had just said. "What?"

Come to the station? It almost sounded like...

"How did she die?" I asked slowly.

"She was murdered..."

I thought a string of profanities. Words I'd never say out loud. Words that would make my father wash my mouth out with soap, despite my adulthood. Then I put on my attorney hat and asked, "And why would I have to answer questions?"

"Her attorney said she fell at the studio and was suing you. That means you have motive." Micci sighed, as if somehow it was my fault a customer fell at the shop. A customer I suspected was a scam artist.

I realized admitting that would only make me look guilty, so I simply said, "I wouldn't kill someone because they fell."

"Why would you kill someone," Micci asked with a hint of a smile buried under her professional cop persona.

I sighed again. "Let me call Micah and have him meet us at the station. And if you don't mind, let me cancel my dinner reservations for tonight."

"Something special?" she asked, looking at my dress.

"Our anniversary."

Micci realized what it being our anniversary meant. "Really? It was a month ago today?"

"Yeah. How the heck did I go from a rather anonymous potter to a woman who keeps finding herself in the midst of murder investigations?" I asked rhetorically.

She shook her head. "I have no idea."

"Me either," I assured her.

I made the call to cancel my reservation first because that was the easier of the two calls.

Then I called Micah.

"Hi," he said. I could hear his smile, which I know sounds absurd, but I could.

"Hi yourself," I said back. I was quiet for a moment, not wanting to wipe the smile from his face.

"I'm on my way over," he said.

"About that..." I did not want to mess up our anniversary with this.

"Is there a problem with dinner tonight?" he asked.

"Yes. You see, Micci's here—"

"Great. Just invite her along," he said. He'd come to look on her as a friend, too.

"No. You see she wants me to come down to the station to answer some questions."

"Questions about—"

"She wants to ask me questions about Velma Harris," I said slowly.

"Isn't that the woman who fell?" he asked. "She filed charges against you? That's crazy."

"No. She won't be filing any more charges. You see, she's dead. Not just dead...murdered."

Micah said the string of words I'd only thought earlier. I heard him take a deep breath, then he said, "You know the drill. Don't say anything until I'm there."

"I do know the drill all too well. I really don't know why this keeps happening to me." That definitely sounded whiny. But seriously, it was my anniversary and I'd shaved my legs in anticipation of the celebration.

What a waste.

"This will be fine," he said, being a boyfriend not a lawyer. "Just like the last time. You didn't do it, so you have no worries."

"Yeah, no worries. See you soon," I said.

I didn't mention it, but I did have worries. Lots of them.

I let out Lily and fed her, grabbed the notebook behind the counter in the shop, then looked at Micci—Detective Dana—and said, "Micah's going to meet us there. Let's get this over with."

Sitting at a police station was absolutely not what I'd planned for the night.

I decided on the drive that I would refer to Micci as Detective Dana again...at least until this matter was cleared up. It seemed better to keep some professional distance between us.

We came in through the lobby. There were white construction paper snowflakes on the reception desk window. I liked that they were ecumenical. They made me feel a little better.

For a second I forgot where I was and thought about making ceramic snowflakes. They could be ornaments or even just window hangings. I could picture them in my mind but real life interrupted my creativity.

We were walking back down a hall I felt I knew too well to the interview room.

"We'll wait for Micah," I said to the detective—I was pleased I remembered to think of her as such—she nodded at me to have a seat.

"Sure," she said. "If it's any comfort, I have a bunch of people to interview."

I knew she was trying to make me feel better, but it wasn't exactly working. "No, it doesn't really make me feel any better."

"I get that," she said. She looked as if she wanted to say more but couldn't. And I got that.

I'd like to just tell her everything right now, but I couldn't.

We'd both been cast in roles we didn't necessarily want to play.

I ran through everything in my mind. I was anxious to see the documents that Velma's attorney was sending. I wasn't sure that they'd help vindicate me, but it would give me more information.

I collected data.

It was why, when I was a practicing attorney, I so enjoyed working on contracts. I loved looking at all the data and figuring out how to put it all together in a way to best protect our client.

I thought about my idea wall that was once again filled with ideas.

I didn't want to replace them with suspects in yet another murder.

There was something about Velma from the get-go that felt off. She was hinky. It felt like she was casing the store. Why?

Given her *almost* falls before she actually managed one, I suspected she'd come in looking for cameras. A camera would kink up her plan. I remembered how she glared at me as I snapped pictures.

I pulled out my phone and looked them over. They were all there. The shot of the shelves and Velma's glare.

It wasn't an expression of someone in pain.

It was the expression of someone who was annoyed.

"What are you looking at?" the detective who used to be Micci asked.

"I'll share it with you as soon as Micah gets here," I told her.

As if on cue, a uniformed officer showed Micah into the interview room. "Wow," he said as he looked at me.

"Wow yourself," I said right back at him. He was wearing a dark suit with a modern cut. I will confess, I didn't know anything at all about suits and cuts, but this was a form-fitting suit...not a slouchy suit like my father was prone to wear. He had a bit of scruff going, which looked good on him. He had this weird piece of hair that was frequently unruly, but today, it was in place. From behind his glasses his blue eyes looked me over, as if to be sure I was okay.

"It's not the night I had planned," I said.

"Me either," he said.

He turned to Micci—darn, Detective Dana. "Why is my client here?"

"Can we have a minute?" I asked her.

She nodded. "I'll be right back."

And so I explained about Velma. I showed Micah our logs, the pictures and said, "Her attorney is supposed to be mailing me settlement papers."

"You weren't going to settle."

"No. But I was interested in seeing what they were after. I'm going to guess he got them right in the mail. Now that the mail goes to Pittsburgh to get processed than back to Erie, it takes longer. But the pictures should help. I didn't want to show them to Micci—the detective—until you were here."

"Yes. But no commenting on your thoughts or feelings. Just the plain, dry facts," he reminded me.

"Yes," I agreed.

"And when we're done here, I'm taking you out," he said.

"I canceled our reservations." I'd really wanted something swanky and romantic tonight.

"We'll go to *Down by the Bay*. You do love their salad. It seems appropriate to celebrate our anniversary there." He was teasing. I'd been doing some amateur sleuthing and used their salad as an excuse and he remembered.

Of course he remembered.

I smiled and then despite being in a police station, I leaned over and kissed his cheek. It was definitely romantic of him to remember. "Thank you."

"For what?" he asked.

"For being here, no questions asked."

He kissed me back, but not a platonic on-the-cheek-kiss. No, his was a kiss that spoke of true and utter desire.

"Wow," I said for a second time that night.

There was a knock on the door and the detective came in. "Ready?"

"Yes," Micah called back.

The detective came in, turned on the recorder and I spit out the facts. *Just the facts*, I thought as I began. I turned over the notebook and emailed her the pictures I took.

"Ms. Harris's attorney called and is sending me settlement papers."

"You were going to settle?" the detective asked.

"I wanted to see what they had in mind. I don't think this was Velma's first slip and fall rodeo," I admitted.

"Slip and fall scams aren't my normal cases, so I've done some research," Micah said. "I made a few calls and found out most people who engage in this kind of behavior don't just do it once. It's a way of life for them. I suspect Velma's done this before. And if she has, then I suspect your suspect list might get very long."

Micci nodded and looked as if she wanted to say something, but she didn't. "Thank you for the information. It will be helpful."

"We'd like the notebook back," Micah said. "You're welcome to make a copy first."

She nodded and left the room with the notebook in hand.

"You've been researching slip and falls?" I asked when the door shut.

"I wanted to know what we'd be up against if she came after you...which she did," he said.

We.

Maybe I should be bristle that he was talking as if this were happening to both of us. A month ago, I'd have definitely had my hackles raised.

Today, it didn't feel as if Micah was trying to take something from me. It felt as if he was trying to share the burden with me.

There was a huge difference between the two.

"Thanks," I said. "What a mess."

"It'll be fine. Did Micci—"

I interrupted him. "I'm sticking with Detective Dana until I'm totally off the suspect list."

He nodded. "Did the detective say anything about when and how Velma was murdered."

"No. She didn't ask for an alibi either." Which was weird.

"I'm sure she'll do that when she gets back."

At which point, the detective opened the door. She handed me back my notebook and leaned over and turned the recorder back on. "Here you go. Thank you for the copies of your notes and the pictures. By the way, where were you last night?"

"Friday nights are my Wine and Mud class. It was our last one until after the holidays." Yay, I had an alibi and a bunch of witnesses.

"Last night at about midnight," she corrected herself.

Shoot. There went my alibi. "In bed I would assume."

"Really? We have a witness who said they saw someone, whose description sounds as if they were describing you, on the west side of town just before midnight," she said nonchalantly, but I could sense she was watching me like a hawk. "Near where Velma lived."

"What witness?" I asked, sure she wouldn't tell me. "It's not true."

"I can't say who," she said.

"Do they have any concrete evidence? A picture? Something on security cameras?" Micah asked.

"No," the detective admitted slowly.

"So it's my client's word versus your mystery informant's word?" he pressed.

"Yes. But given the report and other evidence, I had to interview Harry."

"How did the victim die?" Micah asked.

"I can't release that information at this time," Dana said. "But there was one other thing."

"What?" Micah asked before I could.

The detective looked at me as she slowly said, "Harry's business card, clutched in her hand."

Oh, that didn't sound good.

"It wasn't me," I said. "I think you know that if I'd done it, I wouldn't leave a calling card. But for now, I think we'll leave the interview there. I've given you everything I have. I wasn't on the west side last night."

Technically, my shop and apartment were on the west side of Erie. State Street is our dividing line between east and west. I'd grown up an Eastsider, and that one block wasn't going to change that. And the west side always felt soooo far away, even though I lived there now.

I got up and Micah followed suit.

"Happy anniversary," Micci said, as if she flipped off the recorder. "Sorry this ruined your meal."

"Thanks," I said.

"If you hear anything, call me. Or have whoever you heard it from call me."

"Why don't you give me a few of *your* business cards," I said.

"I'm not asking you to investigate, just if you hear something." She handed me a small stack.

"Right now the only thing I'm thinking about is dinner," I said. It wasn't a promise not to look into this. I knew it, she knew it, and I suspected Micah knew it.

We left the police station. "Let's move my car to your house and walk down," Micah said. It was brisk, but not freezing.

"Sure. I've got to let Lily out before we go."

I woke up my dog to let her outside, then made sure she had food and water. I switched from my heels to boots.

"Sorry," Micah said. "I forgot how awesome you look. I'll drive down."

I shook my head. "No, I could use the air. My coat's long and with boots, I'm ready for whatever the lake dishes out."

This time of year, cold Canadian winds blew over the lake, picking up moisture then dumping snow on the city as they landed. So far this year, the snow had been light. I'd shoveled a couple times, but it really hadn't been much more than a sprinkling.

"When the snow hits, I'm afraid it's going to hit with a vengeance," I said as we reached State Street and turned left, towards the bay.

"I'll keep you warm," Micah said with a chuckle.

I laughed too. "That was sooooo bad."

But for a moment, I couldn't help but think how I'd hoped this evening would end. I took his hand in mine as we walked down to the bayfront and over to *Down by the Bay*. There were holiday lights on the Bicentennial Tower, the big tower that sat on the end of the dock, looking out over the bay, the peninsula, and then Lake Erie.

"I love Christmas lights," I said. "I'm going to buy some after the holidays on sale and go to town next year on my place." I had some lights and a lot of decorations, but I wanted more. There were some things in life that I couldn't get enough of...Christmas was one of them.

"I never bother decorating for the holiday."

I must have made a face because he said, "The city is always so decked out, it never felt like a priority."

Micah smiled at me and I forgot lights. I realized how right his hand felt in mine.

We walked into *Down by the Bay* and there were Christmas lights strung throughout the entire bar.

Trisha was there. We didn't even ask for a table. I followed Micah to two empty chairs at the bar.

Trisha grinned when she saw us. "Hey. How're you guys?"

"Celebrating our one month anniversary," I said.

"You two have the most interesting how-we-met story ever," Trisha said with a laugh. "What can I get you?"

"BREWtal for both of us," Micah said, ordering one of my new favorite local brews. He did know what I liked.

Trisha hurried down the bar to the tap and Micah leaned toward me. "One month. It seems longer." I watched as he realized how that sounded. "I mean, in a good way. As in, I feel like you've always been a part of my life and I like it."

I leaned over and kissed his cheek. "Good save."

Trisha came back with our beers. "Anything else?"

"A salad for me. What kind of soup do you have?" I asked.

"An awesome corn and shrimp chowder."

"Yes, please," I said.

"The same for me," Micah said.

When she left he said, "Happy Anniversary," as he raised his beer.

"Right back at you. I was thinking that maybe tonight we should forget what I said." That had been my biggest plan for this anniversary. Forgetting what I'd said.

"What did you say that we're forgetting?" Micah asked.

"I said I wanted to take things slow."

He inelegantly snorted his beer. "You don't want to take it slow anymore?"

61

"I think we should really celebrate when we get back to my place....unless you don't want to."

"Oh, I want to," he said. "What changed your mind?"

"I've been thinking that a year from now, I might know more things about you. More anecdotes, more childhood stories, but be that as it may, I don't think I'll know you any better than I do right now."

I shook my head. "That came out wrong. I mean, there's knowing a lot of stuff about someone. I knew a lot of stuff about my ex. But that didn't bring us together. It didn't make us close. It didn't save our marriage. I feel closer to you right now than I think I ever felt with him." I took a long drink. "Does that make sense?"

He nodded. "It makes perfect sense to me."

We ate our meals, drank our beer, and talked about everything except for the fact I'd just been questioned about a second murder in a month.

As much as I tried to stay in the moment and enjoy the time with Micah, I kept circling back to the fact that someone said they'd seen me near Velma's. Velma had been holding my card. Velma had been trying to get money from me with a slip and fall claim.

I was involved with a second murder.

At least this time there wasn't a body in my kiln.

New kilns weren't cheap and who would use a kiln that had once fired a dead body? I still had the old one in the garage.

I'd had a number of requests from people who wanted to buy that kiln. It was macabre and I wasn't sure I wanted to sell it to them, but I also wasn't sure what to do with it.

"Harry," Micah said.

I realized that I'd totally lost track of what he was saying. "I'm so sorry. I planned tonight. It was going to be all about you and me and now..."

"Listen, I love the idea of us spending the night together, but I don't think tonight's the night. When we do...get together, I don't want..."

"Another dead body getting in the middle of things?" I supplied.

"Yes," he said with a sigh.

"I can see how that would be awkward," I said, trying to make a joke of it. But it wasn't funny. "I really don't know how this happened."

"You didn't do anything, so just like last time, you have nothing to worry about. You gave Micci—"

I interrupted. "Detective Dana. I like her, but I don't want that fact to get in the way of things. She's investigating me again. Liking her has nothing to do with it."

"This is going to be okay," he said. "Just let the investigation play out...on its own."

I knew that last bit was a warning.

I didn't say anything. Instead I took a large bite of salad—a very unladylike bite that kept me from responding.

"Harry?" Micah said.

When I could I said, "Micah," in the same tone.

"Don't get involved in this one. Velma wasn't in your kiln."

"She did fall at my shop. She was going to sue me, or at least try to scam some money out of me with the threat of suing me. That gives me motive. And given how much my name's been in the press lately, I just want to be sure I'm in the clear."

"*Do. Not. Investigate. This.* Remember what happened last time."

"Yeah, I remember. Do you? I solved the case."

"Not before..." He let the sentence fade, as if he didn't want to remind me of what had happened. "You took years off my life," he said instead.

"Micah, we were just talking about taking our relationship to a new level. I said I didn't need to know all the details of your life to know you. And that's true. But maybe you need to know a detail or two about my life. I don't respond well to orders."

He realized his mistake and said, "I wasn't ordering you, I was—"

"Telling me what to do for my own good. If I subscribed to the idea of doing things for my own good, I'd still be working on contracts at my father's law firm." I'd let my father push me into a legal career, but I'd realized you couldn't really force someone to fit in.

It was like our traditional Christmas jigsaw puzzle. Sometimes from all appearances a piece should fit, but it would be just a bit off. No amount of pushing or squeezing could make that jigsaw puzzle piece fit in a space it didn't belong.

I never fit where my father had wanted me. And I wasn't about to try to fit where Micah thought I belonged.

"Maybe it would have been better if you'd stayed at the law firm," he muttered. "You'd be safe there."

"I'd be slowly dying of boredom, one drip at a time," I said. "I didn't enjoy what I was doing. The whole time I worked there, I don't think I ever woke up and thought, *Darn, I can't wait to go to work today.* Not once. But every day as I walk down those back stairs from my apartment to the studio, I do so with a sense of excitement. I can't wait to go to work. I can't wait to see what the day brings. I love my life. And I think my life is richer with you in it. But that doesn't mean I want you to take control or tell me what to do for my own good. You have to take me as I am."

It was a declaration of sorts.

"This is me. As much as I l...ike you, I won't change who I am for you." I added. I hesitated over how to describe how I felt about Micah. *Like* was a lackluster word, but we weren't at a point where I was willing to say a word with more...luster.

"Harry, I don't want to change you, but I don't want you to jump into situations you're not equipped for. You are not a detective. You're not even an amateur detective. You're an ex-attorney, current potter, potential writer. That doesn't equip you to investigate a homicide."

I took a gulp of my beer. "Agree to disagree."

Micah looked not quite angry, but at least annoyed.

That was okay, because that's how I felt as well. "I think I'd like to go home now."

"Fine." He waved at Trisha and she came down all smiles, then sensing our mood, her smile faded. "Did you want anything else?"

"Just the check," Micah said.

When it arrived, he grabbed it quickly and put his card on it.

I noted what my meal and drink cost after Trisha took his card, I added twenty percent in my head, and dug out the cash. I slid it to him.

"That's not necessary," he said.

"It is. No matter what happens between us in the future, I will always pay my own way and make my own decisions. If you can't handle that, then..."

I just let the sentence hang because I didn't want to think about losing Micah...not after I'd just found him.

"Harry, I don't want tonight to end like this," he said.

"Me either."

No, this wasn't how I'd intended the evening to end at all.

Chapter Four

"Things don't always turn out the way you want in ceramics. You can make two pieces from the same clay, fire them in the same kiln, glaze them with the same glaze and find you have two vastly different results. It's part of the magic of pottery."
~Harry's Pottery

I woke up with a sense of disappointment.

Last night certainly hadn't gone the way I'd hoped it would.

I'd imagined waking up snuggled next to Micah this morning. Instead, I was snuggled up next to Lily.

Now, Lily Potter was a delightful dog and a good companion. Most mornings I didn't mind sharing the bed with her.

Today I did.

I reminded myself it wasn't Lily's fault. "Come on, Lil. I'll let you out and make coffee."

By the time Lily had visited the backyard and had her breakfast, she was exhausted. She curled up on her dog bed.

I took a long sip of coffee. "That's some life, Lil," I said.

I looked at the small tree I'd made for Micah's anniversary present. Well, I hadn't made the tree. I'd found a beautiful white birch branch with plenty of smaller branches. I'd polyurethaned it and made a small stand. I strung tiny LED lights on it. And I'd made a bunch of small ornaments for it. Small round clay discs with holiday pictures. Holly. Trees. Candles. Stars. Snowflakes. I thought they had a folk-art flair. I hoped Micah liked them as much as I did.

I would make a point of giving it to him after we made up.

If we made up.

That was a morose thought to start the day on.

I made short order of getting dressed, then headed to brunch at my father's.

I'd met my soon-to-be stepbrother once, but he hadn't been back to dinner yet. Lucky me...Micah came every week. I wasn't sure if he'd come today.

I couldn't decide if I was still annoyed and hoped he didn't come, or if I missed him and hoped he did.

"Hi, sweetie," Phyllis said when she opened the door. "You know you don't have to knock. This is your home."

Knowing that Dad and Phyllis were going to be married in less than two weeks and would be...intimate. Well, even if I hadn't knocked before, I would now. Some things were not meant for daughters to see.

Ever.

"Thanks, Phyllis."

She put her arm over my shoulder and asked, "How are things at the store? I'm sure you're glad Adi's back."

"It's great." That was a lie, I wasn't. Another murder investigation and a fight with Micah. "And yes, it's good to have Adi home. Thanks again for filling in."

"Any time. I mean it, any time I can help, you let me know."

Dad and Micah were already at the table and deep in conversation about something work related. They both gave me a quick, "Hi," and went on with their discussion.

"Speaking of help, can I help you?" I asked Phyllis.

She allowed me to help carry the roast, potatoes, and carrots to the table.

This was more a dinner than brunch, but Phyllis liked to switch things up and I didn't mind. The meal was awkward. I didn't say much of anything to Micah and he didn't say much of anything to me. Otherwise, we both joined in conversations with Phyllis and my father.

I thought we were doing a good job covering our tension, but I caught Phyllis giving me worried looks. Maybe I was just imagining it.

"There's pie for dessert," she said. "Josiah, would you give me a hand?"

"I can—" I started.

She cut me off. "You sit and relax with Micah. Your father would love to clear the table and help."

I hadn't imagined anything. Phyllis had indeed noticed Micah and I were at odds.

She took a couple dishes back and my father muttered, "Love might be too strong a word." But he smiled as he said it, so I was pretty sure that while he didn't love clearing a table, he did love Phyllis.

When the room was just ours, Micah said, "About last night—"

I shook my head. "Not here."

He tried again. "But I wanted to say—"

I absolutely did not want to discuss last night here. "Please?"

"Later then," he said.

My dad and Phyllis came back into the room. She shot me a look and then sighed, as if she knew Micah and I hadn't solved anything.

Our Sunday brunches had definitely improved since Phyllis came on the scene. She brought out an apple crumb pie with plates and ice cream.

"Phyllis, I'm going to have to diet the rest of the week after Sunday meals here," I said.

"I love to cook. For years it was just me and Dylan. He's a picky eater, so I didn't get to try many things. These Sunday meals have been such a joy to cook for. Thank you again for letting me join you," she said to me.

"Phyllis, you're marrying my father. That means you're family. You belong here."

As I said the words, I realized that it might seem like a cut to Micah, and although I was still annoyed, I didn't want to hurt him. I reached over and patted his hand with mine. Just one brief moment of physical connection. I could see that he understood what I was saying.

It was weird how often we could communicate without saying a word.

"So what's new with you?" my father asked as he passed me a piece of pie.

I saw Micah raise his eyebrow, encouraging me to tell my father.

I shot him a look that I hoped he understood was reminding him about attorney-client privilege.

He shrugged his shoulders, which was him saying, *I can't force you, but you and I both know you need to tell him.*

I sighed, which was my way of saying, *You're right, darn it all.*

The entire non-verbal conversation happened in a split second. I sighed again. "Well, it's been an interesting week."

My father paused, mid-dishing up a piece of pie. "Yes?"

"Well, remember the woman who fell at the store?" That was a lot of wells for just two sentences.

Normally my father would have jumped all over my well-ness, but instead he looked concerned and said, "Yes."

"I was right. Her attorney called and she wanted me to make a cash settlement," I said.

My father seemed relieved that was it. "We can take care of that."

He took a bite of pie and winked at Phyllis. I realized they were speaking without words as well. He'd told her it was delicious.

I wanted to just take a moment and enjoy the fact that my father had found someone, but Micah cleared his throat reminding me that I needed to buck up and get it over with.

"Yes. That's what I thought as well. Only, Micci, Detective Dana, stopped by last night. She wanted to ask me some questions," I said slowly.

"Questions about the slip and fall scammer?" my father asked.

"Yes," I said. I didn't want to do this, but Micah was right. My father deserved to know.

"She's obviously done this kind of thing before," my father said.

"I think so, too. Only, the detective didn't come about her fall," I said, wondering how to say the next part. I didn't ease into, I just said it. "She was murdered."

"Pardon?" my father said.

"What?" Phyllis said, jumping into the conversation.

"Murdered," Micah confirmed.

"Velma Harris was killed," I said. "Dead. She died because someone killed her. Micci's investigating."

"How did she die?" my father asked.

"The detective didn't say, but she seemed pretty sure it was murder."

"How the hell do you get yourself into these scrapes?" my father exploded. He sounded much more like the father I was accustomed to than the father who'd mellowed out since Phyllis.

First Micah, now my dad? It was too much. "Yeah, that's right, Dad. I set out to have a body cremated in my kiln, then I encouraged a customer to fall in my shop and sue me. Then for kicks and giggles, I encouraged her to get murdered just to make my life more interesting. I know, crazy, right?"

He rubbed at his temple. "I didn't mean it like that," he said.

"Harry, it had to have been so scary being questioned again," Phyllis said, trying to be the peacemaker.

"It wasn't scary, it was annoying," I said. "I'm getting dragged into dramas that aren't of my making."

"I hope you're not planning to take things into your own hands again. I think Detective Dana has proven you can rely on her." My father sounded just like Micah.

Or maybe Micah sounded just like my father.

Either way, they both annoyed me.

"You don't need to worry about me," I assured him. "Worry about that wedding." I turned to his fiancée. "Phyllis, how goes the planning? It's two weeks to go."

I saw from her look that she knew what I was doing. When she took off into what amounted to a half hour monologue about their very simple wedding plans, I knew that she was on my side.

When the pie was finished, Dad and Micah started talking about a new client. I assured myself I wasn't sneaking out, but even I didn't believe me. I'd offered to help clean up, but Phyllis assured me she was fine.

"Then I'm going to go," I said. "I have a ton to do for the holiday season. Thank you for brunch...dinner. Thanks for the food."

"It truly is my pleasure," she said. She looked concerned as she added, "And I'll just say, be careful. I'm not going to try to parent you like your dad—"

"And Micah," I added.

"Right. But I will say, be careful. I just started to build this family with your father. I wouldn't want anything to happen to you." She was so sincere and her worry so palpable, I couldn't be annoyed with her.

"I'll be careful, Phyllis. I truly don't think this has anything to do with me," I assured her.

"Good." And then, this woman I barely knew who was going to be my stepmother in a few weeks, hugged me.

Really hugged me.

I was so surprised that I think I hesitated a second too long, but eventually, I hugged her back.

Then I quietly let myself out of my father's house and went home.

I walked through the storefront, and restocked a few shelves.

I was just getting ready to sit at the wheel when my cellphone rang.

I pulled it out of my back pocket and saw who it was.

Normally when I saw Micah's name on my phone, I'd feel a surge of happiness. Today, that was still there, but there was an undercurrent of annoyance wrapped around it.

"Hi, Micah," I said a bit stiltedly as I answered.

"Harry, I didn't get a chance to say goodbye to you." His voice was neutral, as if he were purposefully trying not to scold me.

"Sorry, I have a lot to do here. The next couple weeks will make or break my business year." That was true, but we both knew it was an excuse.

He was quiet a moment, then said, "I just wanted to say I'm sorry."

"Sorry for what precisely?" I asked.

"For trying to tell you what to do," he said.

"You're seriously sorry you told me not to look into Velma?"

His sigh was audible over the phone line. "Okay, no, I'm not sorry for that. I think it's ridiculous to get mixed up in Velma's death. You didn't do anything, so it doesn't have any impact on you."

"She was suing me, then she was murdered. I'm a suspect," I said.

"Not much of one," he muttered.

"This on top of the body in my kiln? It's how people get a reputation. I don't want to be known as a shop where people go to die. The little shop of horrible deaths."

"No one died there," he said, trying to maintain that neutral voice, but I could hear his frustration start to come through. "You're exaggerating. One person was there then died, another died somewhere else and was put in your kiln."

"The pushing up daisies potter," I continued. "The cadaverous ceramicist. The assassination artist. The crafty crafter. The—"

"Harry, you're being a bit dramatic," he interrupted.

His voice wasn't neutral anymore. I was pretty sure I could hear a chuckle in his voice. Not a chuckle because he thought my death quips were funny. Not a laughing *with* me. A laughing *at* me. As if a potter couldn't be an amateur sleuth.

If Quincy Mac—an Erie maid who'd moved to LA—could solve a few murders, so could a potter in Erie.

"Yeah? I'm dramatic? Well, how's this for dramatic?" I hung up on him.

Yes, I know, it was sort of high school. And frankly, it wasn't nearly as satisfying as slamming a receiver in the cradle. I just pushed a button.

I wasn't overly proud of myself.

But after being with my ex for so many years, I knew what I wanted. Someone who would be there for me, no matter what.

I wanted someone who'd have my back if I were under investigation for murder.

Someone who would have my back when I *investigated* a murder.

Micah certainly managed the first, but he was decidedly lacking in the second.

Then I thought about all the other wonderful things he'd done for me in the last month and I started to feel guilty. I didn't tend to be someone who flew off the handle. Micah hadn't tried to be unkind. He'd simply been concerned.

I sat down at my counter and called him back.

He answered with a simple, "Yes?"

"That was juvenile. I'm sorry. I don't think I'm someone who flies off the handle that easily, but obviously sometimes I do. And let me say it again—I'm sorry. You didn't deserve that."

"Apology accepted. And I owe you one as well. I'm sorry. I wasn't trying to control you, just... Okay maybe I was, but not out of any maleficence, or misogynistic reasons. I'm worried about you, that's all."

How can you be mad at someone who's only concern is you?

You can't.

"Let's start over," I said. "Hi, Micah."

He chuckled. "Hi, Harry."

"I got up on the wrong side of the bed this morning and I wasn't overly pleasant at brunch but I'm hoping despite that, you'll come over later for supper. I'll cook."

"Uh..." he hesitated.

"Are you hesitating about coming over because you're still annoyed?" I asked, though I was pretty sure I knew the answer.

He chuckled. "No. I'm hesitating because I know you don't cook."

"Well, cook was maybe too broad an offer. I mean, you had a delicious roast earlier so you've had your big meal of the day. I'll order pizza."

"Then I'm there." He paused a moment. "And Harry, I know whatever we have is in its nascent stage, but let me say I will never try to control you. I will probably always worry about you, at least a bit."

"And if you found a dead body and were under suspicion of murder, I'd worry about you, too," I admitted.

"So, have we made up from our grand fight?" he asked.

I smiled. "Yes. And if that's going to be our version of a grand fight, I think we might be pretty lucky."

He laughed. "Me, too. And I promise, I'll try to be less..."

"Worried?" I filled in.

"Well, I can't promise that, but I'll try not to let it get in the way," he said sincerely.

"Good enough. And I'll try to recognize the difference between concerned and controlling."

"See you tonight," he said.

"Tonight."

I hung up and felt remarkably better. I sat at my wheel and worked on a big casserole dish, humming Christmas songs as I did.

I stared at my idea wall.

Last time, I'd taken the whole thing over as I tried to figure out who put a body in my kiln.

Micah was right. This time didn't seem quite so worrisome. After all, Velma had only fallen here before she'd been killed.

I decided not to take over the whole board. I divided it in half. On the right side, I kept the ideas for the book going.

On the left, I wrote Velma's name on a Post-It.

Then her lawyer, *Shawn Hawkins*. I put a question mark next to his name.

Thinking of him made me realize I hadn't picked up the mail yesterday. I hurried to the box on the porch and there were a few business letters, a lot of holiday junk mail, and one big white envelope. The return address read S.P. Hawkins, Esquire and had a PO Box address here in Erie.

No office?

That was weird in and of itself. When I'd run a search on all attorneys named Hawkins and I knew I'd have remembered an SP.

I opened up the envelope and looked through the papers he'd sent. Growing more and more concerned as I read.

They weren't quite right.

As someone who'd built her short-lived law practice on writing a lot of contracts and proposals, I recognized that the papers in my hand were...*off*.

It's kind of like a student who'd taken French classes for years and aced them all.

Then went to France.

She could make herself understood and even understand most of what was being said, but it wasn't quite right. Any true French person recognized the fact she wasn't French the minute she opened her mouth.

"Merde," I muttered as I went through SP Hawkins paperwork.

They'd wanted five thousand dollars.

Past tense.

Because Velma was dead they'd get nothing.

I thought about the amount.

Don't get me wrong, five thousand dollars is a lot of money. It was more than most small business owners readily had on hand, but not so much that they couldn't find it somewhere.

I thought about my insurance policy. Money is tight with any start up, so I'd kept my deductible high in order to keep the cost of my policy lower. I had a two thousand dollar deductible. So it might be worth it to just pay Velma off in cash and not go through the insurance company and risk them raising my rates.

There.

I spotted a nondisclosure paragraph.

Velma and her attorney wanted me to pay them in cash and then not be able to comment on the fact I paid them.

Yeah, everything about this felt hinky.

If I handled Velma's claim privately and it didn't go through insurance then, when you factored in a nondisclosure element, there'd be no record.

If I were a slip and fall con artist, that's just how I'd want things. With no record readily available. No paper trail for anyone to follow about my activities.

I called Detective Dana. She must have recognized my number because she answered by saying, "Hi, Harry. No, I haven't solved the case yet."

"Neither have I," I teased.

Unlike Micah, she chuckled. Oh, I knew she wouldn't allow me much leeway before she got annoyed, but at least at the moment, she was still amused. Though she did ask, "You're not really trying to solve this one, right? I mean, it didn't happen in your shop."

"I know," I said, not really answering her question. "I got the offer from Velma's attorney. It feels off. I thought you might want to have a copy."

"I do," she said quickly. "Especially if you think there's something not quite right about it."

"Are you at the office?" I asked.

"Yes."

"Tell you what, I'll bring it over so you can make a copy. And since I've decided to ignore the fact you took me to the police station for questioning again, I'll even bring you coffee from *Ember and Forge*."

She laughed. "Great. Just black please."

Lily looked up as I got my coat. "I'll take you later," I promised her.

She plopped back down on her dog bed. I'm not sure she was disappointed. Lily did like a good walk, but she didn't want to do too many. She had limited doggy energy on any given day.

I put the papers in my bag, walked over to State Street, got two coffees and walked the few blocks to the police station.

By now, I knew my way to the reception desk. "Detective Dana," I asked the woman behind the glass window. "She's expecting me."

"I'll get her," she told me.

Moments later, Micci walked through the door. "Come on back."

I handed her a coffee.

"So what seems *off*," she used my word, "about the contract?"

"It's just hinky." I used my French analogy. "There are real legal terms in it, but it's as if someone took a real contract as a template and then added non-attorney conditions. Plus, I couldn't find a Hawkins who was part of the Pennsylvania Bar. It doesn't mean he doesn't have his law license in some other state, but he doesn't have it here. And his office address is a PO Box. Also weird. Even now that I'm pretty much retired as an attorney, if I were sending something out, I'd use Dad's office, or even the shop's address. I wouldn't use a PO Box. And there's no phone number. Everyone's got a cellphone these days. Even if he doesn't practice out of an office proper, you'd think he'd list a phone number."

"Or email," Micci muttered as she looked through the papers.

"Right. It's just off," I said.

"*Hinky*," she added with a smile.

"It's a good word," I said.

I handed her the papers. She leafed through them, set her coffee down and said, "Hang out here a minute. Let me go make copies."

"Sounds good." I drank my coffee and for the first time ever I felt rather relaxed while sitting in a police interrogation room.

I thought about this lawyer, this SP Shawn Hawkins. There was no way to contact him other than mail. When he called, he'd called the shop's number. We didn't bother with caller ID on it. It was a public line.

I pulled out my phone and Googled his name and PO Box, but it didn't get me any further than just his name. I opened Facebook, then Twitter, then searched his name and Erie.

Nothing.

Micci came back in the room and handed me back the originals. "This might help. Thanks."

"Have you talked him yet?" I asked.

She shook her head. "We can't find him either."

"I've been thinking," I said slowly. I took a long sip of my coffee.

"Uh oh," the detective said.

"What if I sent a letter to this attorney's PO Box and offered to make some remuneration to Velma's family? Maybe I feel guilty about the fall? Maybe SP Hawkins would want to meet with me, and if he does, you could show up and talk to him. Maybe you'd find out what's going on."

"I don't know," Micci said. "If this was a slip and fall scam, then odds are he's mixed up in it, especially if he's not part of the PA bar."

"If it is, I can't imagine Velma's attorney would want to kill her. After all, it would be like killing the goose that laid golden egg. He'd be cutting off his financial resource. And as an attorney, let me ask the question...just how dangerous could he be?"

She laughed.

"All right. If you agree that I help you write the letter and you contact me if and when he contacts you."

"Deal. Despite what Micah and my father think, I don't want to be embroiled in another murder investigation. I just want to get back to my normal life. I want to make pottery, teach some classes, and maybe write a book."

"A book?" Micci asked.

I realized I hadn't told her. "Yeah. I got a call from a publisher who's interested..."

"That's awesome." She said when I finished. "As for classes—"

"They won't start up again until after the holidays. So you have a few weeks to figure out who killed Velma so you can come to my class and not have it be a conflict of interest."

She laughed. "Yes, that's the driving force for me behind this investigation for me."

I grinned and nodded. "I know. Your passion to try pottery is why you want to solve this mystery."

We both chuckled, though I wasn't sure it was very funny.

Then we wrote the letter together. Basically, I felt so guilty about what happened and wanted to make a voluntary settlement with Velma's family. We used my cell number, which would give us his phone number at least.

"I'll put it in the mail," Micci said. "And you'll call me..."

"The second I hear from him." I crossed my heart and held up a couple fingers. I was pretty sure it was some sort of scouting sign.

"Right," she agreed.

I went back home and worked. When it was almost dinner, I ordered pizza and Micah picked it up.

"How was your day?" he asked as we ate. I hesitated a moment. How to answer that?

On one hand, I didn't believe in lying.

On the other hand, Micah had confessed he worried about me and I didn't want him to worry more.

I settled for the truth...just the barebones of the truth.

"That settlement offer came from Velma's attorney. I took it to Micci. And went over it with her. I wanted to help her investigation."

"Helping her is a good idea," he said quickly. Too quickly. "The sooner she wraps up this case, the better."

"That's exactly how I feel," I assured him.

I took a huge bite of my pizza. I didn't mention the letter we'd sent Shawn. I felt a twinge of guilt, but I told myself it was for Micah's own good. I was just saving him the worry, because meeting with an attorney didn't warrant any concern.

And I tried to believe I kept it from him for his sake, but even I wasn't buying it.

After dinner we bundled up and took Lily for a long walk. My couch-potato dog did perk up when I got out her lead. We walked down to the bay and stood a moment at the end of the dock. You could see across the black water to the peninsula, where a few lights glowed.

The waves pounded against the dock walls. The glow from the city behind us cast a reflection on the water.

Micah reached out and took my gloved hand in his gloved hand.

And though there was no skin-to-skin contact, I felt connected to him.

"Micah, last night, I'd planned to ask you to spend the night and then..." I let the sentence die, not wanting to rehash anything from last night. "I know you have work tomorrow, but..."

He smiled then. A slow, lazy smile that moved from his lips straight to his blue eyes that were not quite hidden behind his glasses. And I was thankful for the light of the city clearly showing me his pleasure.

"Let's go home," he said.

"Let's go home," I repeated.

Chapter Five

"In ceramics, sometimes something comes out
of the kiln and you realize it's simply magic.
Not because of something you did,
but because magic is in clay's nature."
~Harry's Pottery

I'd slept in the same house as Micah before. But I'd never slept in the same bed.

I thought about last night. It was magic.

Even in my head, that sounded lame, but it was the truth. Being with Micah for the first time hadn't been awkward...it had been right. As if we belonged together.

As if we'd always been together.

I slowly opened my eyes and discovered he was nowhere to be seen.

I got up, tossed on a pair of cut-off sweats and an old Journey t-shirt. They were my version of pajamas.

I went into the kitchen and smiled when I saw him. There he was, sipping coffee and reading something on his phone.

He looked as if he belonged in my kitchen in the morning.

"What're you reading?" I asked as I headed toward the coffeemaker.

"The paper," he said. "They're predicting a lot of snow between now and Christmas."

"Great. After snowmageddon last year, I was hoping for a green Christmas."

"Doesn't look promising," he said and kissed me as I sat down, coffee in hand. "But on the bright side, I can think of worse things than being snowbound with you."

"That was a lovely way to start the day," I said.

He went back to his paper and I took a long sip of my coffee.

Lily was normally dancing around me as soon as I got up, eager to go out and then have breakfast. I realized she was sleeping in her dog bed. "Hey, Lily wanna go out?" I asked.

"She's already gone out and I fed her," Micah said.

Lily raised her head and then promptly plopped it back down again.

Nice.

I sat on a stool at the counter, sipped my coffee and watched Micah read the paper. It was quiet. We didn't need to fill up the silence with noise. And as I sat there, I realized I was more than happy...I was content.

Now, if you asked people if they'd rather be happy or content, I suspect many if not most, would say happy. I mean, happy seems to be the opposite of sad. But maybe, I posited between sips of coffee, being content was better. It was the opposite of discontent. It meant that nothing was actively making you happy or sad, you were just exactly where you were meant to be, and with the person you were meant to be with.

I didn't think about my ex often, but he came to mind now. Not in a wistful, bitter way, but in an I-never-felt-this-way-with-him sort of way. I'd been happy with him. I'd been sad because of him. In between I remembered a lot of frustration. We never felt like we were on the same page at the same time.

But here, at this moment, I was on the same page with Micah. A page I very much wanted to be on.

I reached over and put my hand on his, just needing to touch him.

"What are you smiling at?" he asked, looking up from his reading.

"You. I'm just looking at you and thinking that there is nowhere else on earth I'd rather be than right here, right now with you."

He leaned over and kissed me.

What started out as a friendly, sweet kiss turned into something more.

He took my hand and led me toward the bedroom.

"Don't you have to be to work?" I asked.

"Yes, but I can be a little late."

By the time we were through, I was afraid he was a lot late.

And he didn't seem to mind.

Neither did I.

When he finally got dressed and ready to go, I remembered my anniversary present for him. "I made you something."

I got the small tree with the ornaments.

"I know you said you don't decorate for Christmas, so I made you this. I have the perfect sized box, so all you have to do is plop it in the box at the end of a holiday season and store it. Then just pull it out the next year, plug it in, and you're good to go."

He hesitated a moment, then said, "Thank you, Harry. It's lovely."

I kissed him goodbye again. "Have a good day."

He took his boxed tree and left.

And I went down to my quiet studio. The store was closed on Sundays and Mondays. I had brunch with Dad on Sundays—now with Dad and Phyllis. I hadn't asked if they were living together, but I suspected they were. If not, technically, then in all the ways that counted.

Mondays though...those were my days. I loved how quiet the studio was. There were no customers. No interruptions. Just me and the clay.

I went to work. There was something soothing about the rhythm of ceramics. First, you wedged a hunk of clay, making it consistent and free from air pockets. For efficiency's sake, I did a dozen balls at a time and bagged them. Then I sat at the wheel with a bucket of water and a few tools.

I threw a ball of clay in the center and turned on the wheel. Even though I'd thrown the clay in the center, I still needed to *center it*. I made sure it was as perfectly centered as possible. Then a dropped a hole, opened it up and pulled the walls of the sides up to the desired height.

When I started wheel-throwing class, my instructor wanted us to make six, six-inch cylinders. I could consistently get to five inches, but six eluded me. So I played and fussed and occasionally fumed. Then one day, I just got it. I understood how to pull those walls and make them go higher.

I wasn't perfect yet, but that was the beginning of understanding.

I looked at my idea wall as I pulled a bowl, which did not need to be six inches high as it happened.

When it was done, rather than work on the next, I wiped off my hands, got up and wrote myself a Post-It with my thoughts on pulling walls.

I stuck it on the book side of my idea wall. Then I looked to the left. There was Velma Harris's name and Shawn, SP, Hawkins. I added a Post-It that said *hinky* next to Shawn's name.

I realized that Micci had never mentioned how Velma died.

I didn't get the newspaper, though if Micah was going to stay over more often, I might have to start getting it delivered.

But I could look up the article online as well as Micah could.

I got my phone, plugged *Velma Harris* into the search engine, and found the article.

The body of Velma Harris, 72, of Mauri Road Trailer Park, was found in her RV this morning after a neighbor called about a disturbance and gunshots. The victim was dead when the police arrived. They are awaiting autopsy results and looking for an older, overweight, bald white man. If you have any information, please call the Police...

Though they wouldn't make an official cause of death until after the coroner ruled, it sure sounded as if Velma had been shot. Shot after a loud argument.

If Velma made a habit of slip and fall scams, there might be a trail of victims, any one of whom could be a suspect.

I felt fairly confident that if push came to shove—an unfortunate phrase when dealing with a slip and fall scam-artist murder-victim—I could win in a legal battle with Velma. I'd take notes, I had pictures and knew the law.

But other victims might not have any legal experience and might not be able to afford a lawyer.

I knew how hard starting a new business was. I'd lived and breathed my studio and shop since I'd opened. I'd poured my savings along with my blood, sweat, and tears into it.

Just like I imagined every other small business owner did.

What if you felt someone was threatening all that work? What if they were threatening your livelihood and your family's security?

Yes. Even though I hadn't felt murderous toward Velma, I'd felt angry and I imagined that others in my position would have felt that as well.

The question was, would one of her victims be angry enough to kill her?

If her proposal to me was any indication, Velma avoided insurance companies and actual lawsuits. She relied on private deals and nondisclosure agreements.

There still could be a paper trail out there, even if it was a small one.

I was pretty good at research but I knew my limitations.

I called Coco, my friend who just happened to be a PI. She did a lot of work for my father's law firm.

She'd helped me with the body in my unfortunate incident last month.

I called her again. "Hi, Coco, it's Harry. I have a job for you."

She groaned. I mean, actually groaned a tortured sound. "What have you got yourself into now, Harry?"

"Is that any way to talk to a client?" I countered.

"No," she admitted. "But it is exactly how you should speak to a friend."

I laughed. "This isn't like the last time. At least not exactly."

"Have you been to the police station for questioning?" she asked.

"Yes," I admitted slowly. "But it wasn't like last time."

"If you were at the station being questioned, I'd say it was quite a bit like the last time. Still, shoot."

Shoot. That was an unfortunate word choice.

I told her about Velma, Shawn, about my business card and asked if she could see if she could find out all she could about Velma and added SP Hawkins.

In the meantime, I had an idea on how I could get information on who else Velma had hustled.

I double-checked the papers SP Hawkins had sent me. I was looking for a perpetuity clause...but there was nothing.

That meant anyone else who'd signed a contract like Hawkins had sent me probably hadn't signed a perpetuity clause either.

That meant when Velma died, so did their nondisclosure agreement.

I thought over my plan as I threw the rest of my wedged clay.

Sometimes the simplest plans were the best. And sometimes timing played a huge role as well.

I called Micah and told him I had to go to a meeting...which was the truth.

"Great," he said. "No, I didn't mean it like that. It's just that this case is creeping up and I have so much to do."

I laughed. "I get it. No worries tonight. I'll be out."

"I'll see you...?"

"Tomorrow, unless you're still swamped. And if you are, truly, I understand."

"Thanks." He hesitated, as if he might say more, but finally he just said. "Good night."

"Night," I said as well.

At a little before seven that evening, I cleaned up and bundled up—the skies were grey and looked heavy with potential snow. I headed up State Street.

It was our monthly DBA meeting. The DBA was the Downtown Business Alliance. And I was lucky not only was it meeting night, but it was the Christmas meeting. That meant a pretty good turnout and no actual meeting, just mingling, wine and food.

We were holding it in the Erie Art Museum this year. They had a lovely meeting room that was perfect for our event. And as part of the Downtown Community, they were an integral part of our group.

I came in a bit late, but that wasn't a problem since it wasn't a normal meeting.

"Harry," Darla Greer from *The Music Shop* hollered. "Find any bodies in your kiln?" she asked, laughing.

I rolled my eyes. I reminded myself that I'd found the body recently enough to still be a timely thing.

"Not today," I said. "How about you? Any interesting customers lately?"

"Do you mean anyone who makes me want to sing the *blues*?" Darla laughed at her own music pun. "Or anyone who made my heart *hip-*

hop. Or anyone that made me want to *rap* my head against the wall. Or..."

She was cracking herself and didn't show any sign of having met Velma.

I gave her a weak smile and waved as I headed into the crowd.

I tried to circumspectly ask everyone about Velma. And I got nowhere.

So maybe pottery was a better calling than international spy.

After an hour, I gave up.

I was sitting in a corner, rethinking my ability to track down who-dunnit.

"Hey, why so glum?" asked Adrienne Misty, owner of *Renaissance Woman,* a small shop that had an eclectic mix of products. It was rare that I visited and didn't find something I couldn't live without.

"I am not a super-sleuth," I said.

She laughed. "So you're a lawyer, a potter, but you're no Trixie Belden?"

Despite my despondency, I grinned. "Oh how I loved those books when I was younger."

Maybe that's what this was, my desire to be like my childhood hero.

"Me, too," she agreed. "I'm more into Jenn McKinlay these days. I just picked up her latest one and was hard pressed to put it aside in order to come to the meeting tonight. If it hadn't been the Christmas party, I wouldn't have come."

I laughed. "I've read her books, too. Cupcakes and libraries...I love both."

Adrienne joined in and then grew serious. "What were you sleuthing tonight?"

"I was trying to find out if anyone else had dealt with Velma Harris. She came into the shop and *fell*." I air-quoted the word fell. "I think she's a scam artist."

"If she fell in more than one local establishment, I'd say you might be right," Adrienne said slowly.

Slowly enough that she caught my attention.

"Did she—" I started to ask.

Adrienne interrupted. "If she did, she probably insisted if people didn't want to get sued, they make a cash payment and sign a nondisclosure agreement. Which means if you asked questions, most people wouldn't answer, if they had made a deal like that with her, not that I'm saying I know anyone who made a deal like that with her."

I could have pointed out that she was dead and that after looking at the agreement I was sent, that NDA was no longer an issue, but I suspected that if someone suspected they might become a suspect they might not talk either.

I realized how many times I just thought the word *suspect* and smiled.

"Maybe I've heard that there could be a few local businesses something like that happened to," Adrienne said.

"Such as?" I asked, pretty sure that Adrienne was one of those businesses.

Adrienne just shook her head. "So have you tried *Chili Pepper's*? That new restaurant on State yet?" She didn't say anything else but gave me a look that said the owner of that store might be in our club.

"No, but I'll have to go there soon," I said.

"Yes, you really should. They're fantastic. Tell Cindi Parker I sent you. Pepper—that's what she goes by—is a heck of a cook."

"Thanks. I will." Now that I had another lead, I said, "And Adrienne, if someone was scammed by Velma and signed an NDA, their nondisclosure can't be enforced anymore."

"Why not?" she asked. "My understanding is they don't expire."

"Velma's dead," I said softly. "And I can't believe that person had anything to do with it. So it would be better if they went and talked to the detective and let her know about Velma's hijinks. That kind of information might help her figure out who did it."

I slipped her Micci's card and added, "And if that person needs to talk, they have a friend at *Harry's Pottery* who is always willing to listen.

Adrienne slipped the card in her pocket and said, "Thank you," then hightailed it out of there.

Well, that was a bit better. Two. I was pretty sure Adrienne would be hard pressed to swat a fly, but Cindi Parker? I didn't know anything about this *Pepper*. Maybe she didn't like getting scammed?

Didn't like it enough to murder someone?

I wondered how many other businesses Velma had messed with.

Nondisclosure at work, baby.

I circulated for another hour and then I went home. I was anxious to add two names to my list, *Renaissance Woman* and *Chili Pepper's Restaurant*.

Both were small, local mom and pop sort of business. Rather like *Harry's Pottery.*

And for the life of me, I couldn't imagine Adrienne killing anyone any more than I could picture Adi doing it.

But now I had a clear trail that suggested that Velma *was* indeed a slip and fall scam artist.

Well, not necessarily slip and fall. Maybe she didn't have just one kind of scam. Maybe she'd do anything to make a buck? It seemed to me if you were someone who made money by tricking other people you wouldn't be overly tied to one particular way over another.

Because she was older, slip and falls made sense.

She could have fallen in a restaurant, but she could have done something to the food. Oh, that would be a good one. *Find* something gross or dangerous in your food and threaten to take to the board of health or the newspaper. That kind of press could ruin a small business.

I stared at my board a while longer, then got my laptop and looked up small business scams. Wow.

People who showed up with non-existent order invoices and demand that an employee pay from the register seemed to be popular. Some of the digital scams didn't seem to be up Velma's avenue. She seemed more of an in-person scammer. There were all kinds of hotel scams. People who *hurt* themselves on needles and other implements supposedly left by previous guests. Restaurant scams were voluminous. And...

It was depressing.

I couldn't understand why anyone would feel this was a good way to make a living.

I stared at my wall for a long time, until my phone buzzed.

It was Micah. He texted. *See you tomorrow?*

Yes. Dinner at Down By the Bay?

It's a date. I'll stop by your place first.

Just meet me there.

I hadn't asked anyone at our favorite restaurant. Maybe Trisha would be working. I was pretty sure she'd tell me what she could if Velma had visited.

I busied myself with making more notes about the book and populating that side of my idea board with more...well, ideas.

As I scribbled notes, I put aside thoughts of Velma and scams and concentrated on the best way to communicate an art form in writing. Art was so subjective. Not only what people liked as an individual, but what they made as artists.

I made a lot of functional pottery because that sold best in my store and I was a working potter, which meant those sales had a direct correlation to my ability to eat.

But in my heart of hearts, I loved hand-built, carved pieces. I'd sold one of my most expensive pieces ever just a few weeks ago, *Dyad Emerging*. A dyad literally emerging from a tree. I'd spent hours upon hours carving it, plus hours glazing and staining. I put an absurdly high price on it because, to be honest, I didn't really want it to sell. I'd actually felt slightly upset when it sold. And a bit shocked that someone would pay that much for something I made.

I printed a pic of Dyad from my laptop and put it on the board.

That.

If I wrote a book—and truly it was still a big *if*—I wanted to talk about the balance.

Balancing running the business with making the art.

Balancing making pieces that sold readily with pieces that touched my artistic heart.

Balancing work and family. Balancing work and friends.

Balance.

If I wrote a *Harry's Pottery* book, that would be my underlying theme.

I wrote the word in marker and posted it in the center of the board.

I didn't know that I'd ever need to state the theme, but as I worked on ideas for, and possibly later worked on actually writing a book, that would be how I'd put it all together.

Balance.

I looked at my board and found it was balanced between Velma and the book. Last time, the investigation had eaten up the entire board. It had eaten up everything.

This time it was better because there was balance.

I think last time I felt a greater sense of urgency since the body had been in my kiln...in my studio.

Even though Velma had threatened my business, it wasn't quite as close to home.

Not after I'd found two more people she'd scammed.

From what I'd read, people who used slip and falls scams didn't do it just once. They didn't do it a couple times. For most of them, it was a way of life. In truth, it was their job.

That's what I was for Velma...a job. Something that would lead to a payday.

I felt that I would have stood a good chance at winning if she'd pursued her case after I didn't pay. Because I wouldn't have paid.

But what if someone else she scammed didn't have a law degree? What if someone else felt their business was threatened?

Was that enough of a motive to murder someone?

Fear.

Yes. That seemed like a powerful motivator.

But how was I going to figure out who?

It was a puzzle.

And suddenly, that Christmas jigsaw puzzle upstairs lost all its appeal.

Maybe that's why I was so intrigued by Velma's story. It was a puzzle and I loved puzzles.

Chapter Six

"Pottery is the ultimate puzzle. Figuring out how to make something that's in your head move from ethereal to reality is part of it."
~Harry's Pottery

The next night, I spotted Micah in *our* seats at *Down by the Bay.*

Yes, after being a nerd my entire life, I finally had a seat at the bar. As I walked in, Trisha hollered, "Hey, Harry."

It was my *"Norm"* sort of greeting and it made me smile.

"Hey, Trisha," I hollered back.

"The usual?" she asked.

I nodded and she gave me a thumbs-up. I walked up to Micah and kissed him full out on the mouth.

"So how was your day?" he asked as I sat on the stool.

"Busy. I was happy with sales during last year's holiday season, but this year it's exponentially higher. I suspect it's my current notoriety." The thought took some of the wind from my sails.

"Or the word has gotten around that you are an amazing artist and people are coming because of that."

That was exactly the right answer. I kissed his cheek as Trisha brought me a

BREWtal. I still adored Guinness, but I really loved this local beer.

"Hey none of that, you two," Trisha teased. "Keep the PDA to a minimum...that's my motto. Frankly, I'm not sure I'll ever be PDAing again."

I reached out and put my hand on her arm. "When the right one comes along, you'll PDA. Promise."

She shot me an exasperated look. "Young love," she scoffed, then hurried down the bar. But before she went I could swear I saw something like hope in her expression. I knew her ex had hurt her. Maybe she was finally recovering.

I looked at Micah and realized I'd totally healed from the pain my ex had inflicted. I felt as if I were right where and with whom I belonged.

"I missed you," Micah said. "If I wasn't afraid Trisha would yell, I'd PDA all over the place."

"I missed you, too. How's the trial prep going?" I asked.

"Good. I'll be ready. Have you been behaving yourself?" He gave me a very lawyerly look that said he already knew the answer. My father had mastered the look. As a contract attorney, I'd never really had to perfect it which was good because I wasn't sure I had it in me.

"It was only one day. How much trouble can I get into in one day?" I asked, teasing not fighting.

"Do you really want me to answer that?" Micah said, also teasing not fighting.

I laughed and answered, "I went to a DBA meeting last night. The downtown business community can definitely party. But I behaved."

"No more investigating?" he asked as he took a long drink of his beer, as if dealing with me required fortification.

"Nothing directly," I said, which was the truth.

"What does that mean?" he asked slowly.

I wanted to change the subject, so I said, "I figured out something about myself today."

Micah sighed and let me. "What did you figure out?"

"I enjoyed—no, that's not the right word." I mulled it over a moment and then said, "I was drawn into the investigation last month because it was a giant puzzle. I love puzzles."

"I saw that jigsaw puzzle in the living room. All white with a red dot in the center? It's sadistic."

"It's a tradition. My mom started it. Every year, at Christmas, we'd pick a puzzle and put it together as a family. I might be hesitant to try to continue the tradition. I mean, some women might not want to continue a tradition that their husband's first wife started, but I don't think Phyllis will mind."

"I think you're right. She's truly one of the sweetest women I've ever met. She mothers everyone at the law firm. I don't think she's the type to be threatened by a tradition that started before she became part of the family." He gave me a look as if he were seeing something I didn't mean to show him. "So about puzzles?"

"I know I looked into the body in the kiln because it directly impacted me, but in a way it was like a big puzzle. I liked the challenge of trying to figure it out."

"Are you saying that you're going to try to figure Velma out, too?" His concern was apparent.

I shrugged. "She was murdered. I was her most recent victim."

That stopped him. "Wait, there were other victims?"

"I might have asked around at the party last night. I figured people were more likely to talk to me than to Micci. There are at least two other businesses who were targeted, I'm pretty sure. I'm going to go to lunch tomorrow at *Chili Pepper's* to see if I can find out anything."

"How do you know?" he asked.

I shook my head. "I don't have proof, but I have a good lead."

"We could have gone there tonight when I could go with you." There was an undercurrent of annoyance in his voice, as if we might be revving up an argument, which was the last thing I wanted.

"Yes, but dinner is always so much busier. I thought a quick lunch break might be less so and give me more time to talk to the staff, or Pepper if she's there."

"I don't like it." Yep, that was definitely annoyance.

"I'm just eating," I said. I hesitated a moment and added, "And maybe asking a few questions if I have the opportunity."

He ran his fingers through his hair and pushed his glasses higher on his nose with more force than was necessary. "You are going to give me grey hair."

I reached over and touched the hair near his ear. "You already have a bit of it."

"I know. I—"

"I like it."

He smiled. "You're not going to listen, are you?"

"How about this. How about I ask Micci to join me?"

"Seriously?" he asked, as if he thought I would lie to him.

"I don't lie," I reminded him. "I don't think I'm at the top of her suspect list, and after she finds out Velma scammed other local store owners, I think I'll be further down that list. It makes sense."

"Pinky swear?" He held a pinky out.

I hooked mine around his and said, "Pinky swear. Watch." I picked up my phone and texted Micci. *"Hey detective. Any chance you can meet me for lunch tomorrow? I have a couple things to discuss."*

"When? Where?" she texted back almost immediately.

So Micci Dana wasn't much for flowing texts. *"One. Chili Pepper's."*

"I'll be there."

110

I turned the phone to Micah. "Feel better?"

He took a sip of beer, then answered slowly, "A bit. I'll still worry."

I kissed his cheek. "No worries. I'm just doing a bit of poking around. Not really investigating."

He nodded.

I wasn't sure he believed me.

I wasn't sure I believed myself.

Like that all white jigsaw puzzle with the red dot, I really wanted to figure out how all these pieces fit together.

I got to *Chili Pepper's* early.

A half hour early.

I thought my chances of learning something from Pepper were greater if Micci wasn't around.

The restaurant was cute. I couldn't believe I hadn't been here yet. It had been open a little more than a month.

Cindi Parker, aka Pepper, had done a great job on it.

A young woman wearing jeans and a Chili Pepper's t-shirt brought me a water and a basket of homemade tortilla chips and salsa. "Hi, welcome to Chili Pepper's. Can I get you something to drink? Put in your order? I know a lot of people who stop in at lunch are under a time constraint."

"I'm waiting for a friend," I said. "But I'll take an unsweetened iced tea while I wait."

"Got it," the server said.

"Is Pepper in?" I asked before she left.

"A better question is, is Pepper ever not in?" she answered with a laugh.

I knew that feeling. Living over my studio meant I never technically left work. "I've got a shop in the neighborhood, and if she has a moment, I'd love to introduce myself."

"Which shop?" she asked with a smile.

"*Harry's Pottery*," I said.

"The place where..." She let the sentence die, obviously not wanting to offend me. She had that deer in the headlight look, as if she wasn't sure what to say next.

I nodded. "Yes, that's me."

"I'm sorry," she said.

"It was awful, but it's over," I assured her and myself. The unfortunate incident was over and Velma wasn't the same. I was just helping out.

She nodded. "I'll tell Pepper you're here."

The chips were still warm...and delicious.

My server came back with my iced tea and said, "Pepper will be out in a few minutes."

I was mid-bite when a small woman with a huge grin came out and sat in the seat across from me. "Hi. You must be Harry. I'm Cindi Parker, but everyone calls me Pepper. It's so nice to meet you."

"Hi, nice to meet you as well. I wish you'd have been at the DBA party," I said.

"I know. I meant to be, but things got crazy here. And you know how it is. Crazy can be good, and it does make life interesting. A small business takes a big chunk of your life."

"Oh, I know. I have a friend who comes in to work for me on occasion. She's manning the shop now. I find that giving myself a break makes me better at work." It was a hint. Everyone needed a break.

I thought of the book and knew that needed to go in there. *Too much of anything— even a good thing—was too much.*

"Maybe a bit farther down the pike." She chuckled.

"I wanted to ask you something," I said. It was better to just come right out and say it rather than beat around the bush. "I heard there's a chance you know Velma Harris."

The laughter and smile died on Pepper's lips. "Do you know her, too?"

"She *fell*," I air quoted the word, "at my place and she wanted me to pay her off."

Pepper looked as hot as the food she was nicknamed after. "She *found* a fly in her fried ice cream." She air quoted the word *found*. "I had to comp her meal and pay her a hundred dollars out of the till. We both knew it was a lie though. First off, the fly wasn't fried, so there's that. And secondly, she kept saying that one bad *Yelp* review was going to kill a new business like mine. She knew that from personal experience. I've worked too hard to have some con artist destroy it all."

I nodded. "She's dead and—"

"Karma's a bit..." She stopped herself. "That was awful. I'm still furious about the incident, but I don't wish death on anyone."

"Murdered."

Pepper stopped and gave me a look. "And you think I did it because of a fly and a hundred dollars."

I had just met her, but Pepper didn't strike me as the murdering type. Kick your butt? Sure. She was tiny, but I suspected she would be formidable in a fight. Still, I just couldn't see it.

"No. But I think if she came after you and me, she went after others. And maybe one of them was taken for a whole lot more than a free meal and pocket money," I said slowly.

She nodded. "You're right. How can I help?"

"I have a friend meeting me. She's a detective. She investigated me for the unfortunate incident last month."

I remembered my first impression of Micci wasn't quite as favorable.

"Detective Dana's good," I said. "She wants the truth. If you don't mind telling her what happened to you, it could help her start to see a pattern."

"Sure," Pepper said. "I got nothin' to hide. Unless the old broad was killed in the middle of the night, I'm here. All day, every day. I've got alibis out the whazzo."

"I—"

I didn't get any further. Micci came in and took a seat between Pepper and me. "Hey, Harry. And..."

I introduced them. "Detective Micci Dana, this is Cindi Parker. Pepper. She's the owner of the restaurant."

Micci nodded. "Pleased to meet you."

"Harry thought you might want to hear about my dealings with Velma Harris." In short order, Pepper had filled Micci in. "I can probably get an alibi if you need one. But I didn't kill the old broad over a hundred bucks."

Micci nodded. "How about midnight on the seventh?"

"I'm sure I was here. I don't think I've made it home before two since I opened this place. Who am I kidding, since *before* I opened this place. I did most of the renovations myself," Pepper said.

I understood that pride. Although I'd hired out a lot of my renovations, I'd overseen them and did a number of the smaller projects myself.

I looked around the restaurant and smiled. Pepper had strung light up chili peppers with regular Christmas lights. There was a tree in the corner, decorated with not only chilis, but other Mexican themed decorations. On either side of the tree were a menorah and a kwanza kinara.

I smiled at Pepper. "The place looks great."

"Thanks," she said.

Micci nodded and said, "I'd appreciate a few names of people who were working with you that night, just to be sure I've crossed my T's and dotted my I's."

"I'll go check the schedule and get you the names." She got up and without another word, started to the back of the restaurant.

"Is this why you invited me for lunch?" Micci asked.

"I've been asking around, not in a Quincy Mac sort of way, but rather in a helpful sort of way. And like I suspected, I wasn't the only one Velma targeted."

Micci shot me a wry smile. "I had figured that out on my own."

I smiled. "I figured you'd figured, but I thought talking to someone in a non-intimidating way might prove helpful."

"Are you saying I'm intimidating?" Rather than insulted, Micci looked pleased.

I laughed.

She said, "Your friend from Renaissance Woman called this morning, so I was going on a very big hunch today had something to do with that."

The waitress came back. "Hi. Welcome to Chili Pepper's. Can I get you something to drink?"

"Unsweetened iced tea," Micci said.

"And can we have a few more chips? I think I ate my share and Micci's," I said.

The waitress laughed. "Sure thing."

"So you're still poking around this?" Micci asked.

"Not really poking. Just..." I stopped because I was definitely poking and both of us knew it.

Micci just shook her head. "Have you heard back from the lawyer?"

"Not yet, though I'm sure I will," I said.

"And you'll call me immediately?" she asked.

"I will." I held up my fingers in a scout sort of pledge. I'd never been a scout. I had been in Model UN, but we didn't have any pledges there.

The waitress brought back Micci's iced tea and more chips. And towards the end of our meal, Pepper came out with a list of names and numbers. "Sorry, I got sidetracked. I wanted to get these to you before you left. I didn't do anything to her."

"Thank you," said Micci, taking the list. "Do you know of anyone else who had problems with Ms. Harris?"

"I'm not a snitch, but I don't. I'm very new to the business community here and don't have many friends. And those I do have aren't close enough to say, *hey what about this old scam artist?*"

Micci nodded. "If you do hear anything, give me a call?" She handed Pepper a card.

"You bet. And as awful as she was, I hope you find who did it." She sounded sincere and that made me like her even more.

"I will," Micci promised.

I didn't say anything, but silently added my own *I will*.

I'd already brought Micci information she hadn't had before. Maybe I could help her out with more.

"No," Micci said, when Pepper bustled off.

"No, what?" I asked innocently.

"No, I don't want, nor do I need, any more help from you." She sounded like Micah.

"So you're admitting I was a help?" I might not have spent my legal career in a courtroom, but I occasionally managed a good question.

Micci tried to look stern, but I could see an un-coplike twinkle in her eye. "I'm admitting you're interfering in an investigation and that could get you in some legal trouble."

"But I helped," I said again.

She sighed. "Harry, you're a potter. I'm a detective. Let's not confuse the issue."

"Micci, you signed up for lessons, so you—a cop—will be learning about pottery. I guess there's no reason a potter can't learn about investigating." That was a good point, I told myself.

"No," she said simply.

"Okay." I crossed my fingers as I said the word.

The waitress came back with our check and a to-go box.

"Do you mean that?" Micci asked when she left.

I shrugged. "I mean, I sort of signed on to help you find Velma's lawyer, so I am planning on more helping, just to be honest."

Micci sighed.

I took another chip. It was room temperature now, but still so good.

"Listen," she said. "Just promise me you'll call me when the lawyer calls you?"

"I have promised and I will. Seriously, Micci, I don't want to find myself in a situation like last month ever again. I truly just figured I'd get more information from local owners than you would."

She sighed again. "You're right. I'm not sure they would have come and talked to me. But that was enough help. I've got to go."

She threw down bills that more than covered her half and a healthy tip.

I did the same.

"Thank you," I said to the server. And I waved at Pepper. "Come over to *Harry's Pottery* sometime when you take a break."

She laughed.

I changed the invitation. "Okay, come over sometime when your employees need a break from you."

"Now that is a distinct possibility," she said. "I will."

My server called out, "We'll kick her out sometime soon."

I walked home from *Chili Pepper's*. I loved looking down State Street to the bay. I missed the summer boats, but I knew soon the bay would freeze and be covered with fishing huts. I don't know that I had the wherewithal to sit in a shack fishing through a hole in the ice, but I did love watching them start to appear on the bay. I loved seeing the ice fishermen trudge across the ice, some with little sleds.

It was cool today, but I didn't mind. I walked in all weather. And that was the nice thing about Erie's downtown, it was very walkable. It was only a few minutes later that I walked back into Harry's Pottery.

Adi was at the register with a customer. When the woman left with a huge shopping bag, Adi said, "How was lunch?"

I held the bag aloft. "Find out for yourself. Consider it a bonus."

"A bonus is eating without Nori around. She's recently decided everything I cook is gross. I don't think she's human. Really. I love her, but she held off on her terrible twos...until she turned four. I laid out her clothes and told her to get dressed this morning because grandma wanted to take her for the day. She looked me square in the eye as she said, '*I don't want to wear those clothes. I'll dress myself.*' I let her and ten minutes later she came out wearing a princess dress, cowboy boots and a Davy Crocket hat. I asked if she was a cowboy princess. She said, 'No, *I'm Nori.*'"

"I'm not sure that's terrible twos or fours as it were. I think you've raised a self-assured daughter who knows what she likes—".

"Not my food," Adi mumbled between her bites.

"But there's something to be said for that," I continued.

Adi sighed. "I know. When you say it like that, I feel proud. Like despite everything that's happened in her young life, I'm doing okay by her. But when we're in the middle of a battle of wills, it's just frustrating." She reached in the bag and took a chip out. "These are good."

"Did you make Nori change?" I asked.

"No. She was absolutely correct...she was dressed like Nori. My mother wasn't impressed, but she rarely is." She sighed and ate another chip.

From the little Adi had said about her mom, I'd gathered her mother was not an easy woman.

"I hope she didn't give Nori grief," I said.

"We laid the ground rules shortly after Nori was born. My mother can say what she likes to me, but she can never say any of Mom-Classics to Nori. She can't comment on her clothes, or the month Nori decided she was going to braid her own hair, or...any of it. My mom loves Nori enough to try to follow that rule. But she doesn't like it."

I looked at Adi with even more admiration than I'd felt in the past. She was an amazing woman and an even amazinger mother.

Was *amazinger* a word?

I smiled and said, "Any time you need a reminder that you're doing a good job, let me know. I'm in awe of everything you do. You work at your programming job so you can be home with her and fill in here—"

"Mainly to get an occasional adult conversation." She laughed, trying to minimize what she did for me.

I wasn't going to let her. "It's more than that and you know it. You are an integral part of the shop. If I had the money, I'd hire you fulltime and tell you to forget the other job, but I can't yet. I still love that you're willing to help in the piecemeal way I can afford. And last month..."

I didn't need to say any more about it because she knew and I knew. She nodded and took my hand. "I feel like I'm a part of the store. I've learned so much working here. I can talk about glazing techniques and symmetry. I can talk about individual aesthetics when it comes to art. I've always been a geek. Science. Numbers. Programming. They're all concrete. 1 + 1 is always 2. But art? It's intangible. What appeals to one person won't necessarily resonate with another. Art is like magic. And after a lifetime of concrete facts, a bit of magic is welcome."

She just echoed one of my thoughts for the book. "Thanks, Adi."

"Thanks, Harry." She paused and asked, "So did you get anywhere on your new case?"

"What new case?" I asked, trying to sound innocent.

She snorted and just looked at me.

I sighed. "I discovered Velma didn't just play her games at our store. She was working her way through the city, scamming people. I know of a few people downtown, but I'm guessing that she scammed more than that. When you add in the other parts of Erie, and then Harbor Creek, Millcreek, Wattsburg, Corry... There's a lot of fodder nearby. She could have been grazing on it for a long time. And that means the suspect list is vast."

"The people you've found that she scammed...do you think any of them would have killed her over it?"

I thought of Adrienne and Pepper and shook my head. "I get the feeling that she isn't someone who got too greedy. If she made too big of a claim, people would have to go through their insurance. So she kept it big enough for her to survive on, but small enough that even small business owners could afford the loss out of pocket..."

I mulled that over a moment and then added, more to myself than Adi, "Which means, the odds of one of her victims being the killer goes down...way down. I would never kill anyone over a few thousand dollars."

"Uh, what would you kill someone over," Adi asked with a grin.

I realized that we were both at a point where we'd at least started to move beyond last month. "I can't think of anything that would make me murder someone."

"I can," she said softly and seriously.

That got my attention. "Pardon?"

"If someone tried to hurt Nori, I'd do anything to stop them."

I didn't need to think about it, I just nodded. "I'm not her mom, but me too."

"So why would someone murder? Maybe you should mull it over."

I loved that she used the word *mull*. It's a word I used a lot. I thought mulling was as much a part of ceramics arts as working with the clay. Figuring out what you wanted to do, then figuring out how to do it...it was important.

I'd have to add the word to my book Idea Board. Mulling. It was important in art...and maybe in solving a murder.

"Thanks," I said.

Adi nodded. "See you Friday unless you needed me sooner. It's time to go rescue Nori from my mom."

"Good luck. "

A half hour later, I stood in front of my board mulling.

Why did people murder? I'd asked myself that question before. Much too recently for comfort.

People killed for love/hate, to keep a secret, greed, revenge...

There were many others, but these seemed to be the main ones and a lot of the other reasons could actually fall into one of these categories. I put love and hate together because those were different sides of the same coin.

With Velma, it felt as if that idea of revenge might be the obvious choice. But I just couldn't seem to make it make sense. We weren't dealing in millions of dollars, at least not from what I'd seen. But that idea of keeping a secret?

Velma had shown that she was morally bankrupt. She'd do anything—lie about anything—to make a dime. What if she found out something about someone? Something they didn't want to come out? I would have to imagine she'd try to make money on that. She'd blackmail them.

I got a Post-It and wrote, *Secret*?

Micah rang the doorbell. I didn't need to check my phone to see who the app said was at my door...I knew it was him.

I opened the door and asked, "How was your day?"

"Busy, but I think I'll be ready on Monday." He kissed me. "How was your day?"

"Busy, but good."

His eyes narrowed and I could imagine him cross-examining someone on the stand. That look would compel them to answer honestly.

"How was lunch?" he asked slowly.

"Micci came," I assured him.

That gaze eased up and he seemed to relax. "Ah, so she's Micci again, not Detective Dana?"

"I'm pretty sure she doesn't think I'm a suspect," I admitted.

"Ya think?" He started toward the back stairs. "Come on...I'll make you dinner."

I was hungry, but... "Yes, we could do that. Or we could call in an order and find some way to kill an hour while we wait for the delivery."

He laughed. "Sometimes I like how you think."

"Is this one of those times?" I teased.

He nodded. "Yes."

We ordered Thai.

It took a little more than an hour to arrive.

We had no problem filling the time.

Chapter Seven

"In that first ceramics class, I made a Kiln Goddess. Her job was to protect the ceramics in my kiln. All those school years and years as a lawyer, she looked after me. When I got my own studio, she assumed her proper position of looking after the kiln. I suspect watching a kiln was easier than looking after me."
~Harry's Pottery

Micah had told me he wasn't coming over the next night. He had some last minute preparations for his trial.

I got that.

I thought I'd spend a quiet evening working and maybe thinking about the book...but then the phone rang. I didn't recognize the number, but I picked up anyway. "Hello?"

"Is this Harriet? Or do you prefer Harry?" asked a male voice.

"Yes," I said monosyllabically and not commenting on my name.

"This is Shawn Hawkins, Esquire." There was a pomposity in his voice. As if I should be impressed with his *esquiring*.

I wasn't.

I was an attorney. I was raised by an attorney. I was dating an attorney. I knew many attorneys who used *Esquire* in their signature, but I'd never known one to keep using it like this. I was struck anew by how not-quite right Shawn was.

"I received your letter and I was touched. I shared it with Velma's family." He paused. "I know you said you wanted to do right by her family. If you have a check for them, I can meet you tonight to collect. I'll deliver it personally to the family before I leave town."

I grabbed a piece of paper, ready to take notes.

"You're leaving town? Giving up your practice?" I asked.

He hesitated. "I'd been liquidating my interests here in Erie for a while," he said slowly.

"Where did you want to meet?" I asked. "Your office?"

There was a big pause before he slowly said, "Like I said, I've liquidated my assets here in Erie. I could meet you somewhere downtown. Velma's family will truly appreciate of the help. They've been scrambling to pay for her very small funeral."

"Did the coroner release the body?" I asked.

"Yes." That one word was curt and tinged with annoyance. I realized I'd probably exhausted my ability to question him without arousing his suspicions.

I scrambled to think of where to meet. I didn't need to scramble long.

I said, "I'll meet you at *Down by the Bay* in an hour."

"Fine. I'll see you there." He hung up and I realized he hadn't asked how he was going to recognize me. Why would that be? We'd never met in person.

I called Micci. She didn't pick up. I got her voicemail. I left her a message and told her that because I'm not foolish, I'd reschedule.

I tried to call Shawn Esquire back. It went to voicemail at his number as well.

I was stuck. So I called Micci back and went straight to voicemail again. I left a message. I gave her the specifics of my talk with Shawn and where we were meeting. Since I couldn't cancel with him, I'd take the meeting in that very public place. But if she got this in time, I hoped she'd come down.

Then I let Lily out and left.

I was down at my favorite restaurant and bar fifteen minutes later.

"Hey, Harry," Trisha called as I sat down. "Micah on his way?"

"Not tonight. He's working late. Any chance I can get a beer and salad?"

She grinned. "Every chance in the world."

Moments later, she brought my beer. "It looks awful out tonight."

"It was a cold walk down," I agreed, then took a sip of my beer. "But this helps."

She laughed. "You could drive."

"I could, but one of the reasons I love living downtown is I can walk to almost everything. It's my way of staying healthy and saving the world."

Before she could walk away, I added, "Would you do me a favor?"

"If I can you know I will."

"I have someone meeting me here and I need some pictures of him, but I don't want him to know that I want some pictures of him, so I was hoping you could snap a few?"

She gave me a suspicious look. "Harry, just what sort of trouble are you in now?"

"Not trouble exactly."

She just gave me a look.

"Let's just say this is a police sanctioned meeting."

"That does not make me feel better." She shook her head. "I'm going to have 911 on speed dial."

"It's not like that. But you'll take the pictures?"

She nodded reluctantly.

"Please take a bunch," I said. "As close as you can get without being noticed. I just want to be sure we have a good one."

If Micci made it, that was good. If not, I'd have a picture for her at least.

"Seriously Harry, just what are you up to with this police-sanctioned meeting?" Trisha asked, looking at me suspiciously.

"I'm meeting another attorney. I want a picture for my records, but he might think that's odd, so having you take it makes things less awkward."

She frowned. "Less awkward for you, maybe."

I gave her my best *please* look.

Trisha sighed. "Fine."

Almost on the dot, a man wearing plaid slacks and an off white fisherman sweater and dock shoes stood in the door, scanning the bar. It was a Thursday night, so it wasn't weekend crowded.

I gave a small wave and he smiled and made his way toward me. "Harriet?" he asked.

"Shawn?"

He nodded. And his dark hair flopped in a way that let me know it was a comb-over. He was pale and there was a ruddy flush to his cheeks that made him look as if he drank.

Drank too much.

"Have a seat," I offered.

He took the seat next to me. "I can't stay. I just came to pick up your check for the family."

"Oh, have a drink first." I waved at Trisha and she came over. "Can you get my friend a…"

"Guinness," he said.

"Sure," Trisha said as she hurried back down the bar, shooting me a look of concern.

"So where are you moving to?" I asked in a chatty sort of way.

"I'm not sure. I'm thinking about spending a few months just traveling the country. I have an RV and wandering spirit."

Ahhh. If he lived in an RV that would explain why I couldn't find an address for Shawn.

"Have you had it for a while? I've always thought traveling in an RV would be fun." That was a lie. The idea of driving something that big gave me the heebie-jeebies. I drove once a week to grocery shop with Miss Betty. Most weeks that was the extent of my driving.

Shawn nodded. "It is truly wonderful. You can pick up and go whenever you want, wherever you want. That kind of freedom is amazing."

"It sounds amazing." He seemed relaxed. Relaxed enough that I could ask a few more questions. "Can you tell me more about Velma? I know her death wasn't my fault, but I'm so sorry there was a shadow over her last days because of her slip and fall."

"She didn't blame you," he said. Sadly, he shook his head. "Velma had a hard life."

The Velma I met didn't seem like a sympathetic person, but maybe there was more to her than a slip and fall con artist.

"Tell me about her family," I said.

"She has—had," his voice broke a little. "She had a son. The boy's father left when he was still an infant and Velma raised him on her own. She worked hard trying to keep a roof over their heads. She could be a...complicated woman, but she managed to keep him fed."

I nodded, hoping encouragingly. "You sound as if you know the family well."

"I'd done some work for Velma in the past. I like to have a personal connection with my clients. That's why I've always worked on my own. I can give them time and build personal connections that a big firm can't. It's my hallmark."

Trisha interrupted as she brought Shawn his beer.

He took a long, deep drink. "The perfect drink."

"I love Guinness, too. I've been drinking BREWtal lately. It's a local stout. They named it after that big storm last winter. Were you here for that?"

He took a long sip of his Guinness. I suspect it was his attempt at not answering me. So I just said, "You'll have to give it a try."

I wanted answers, but I didn't want to spook him.

"I'll have to try one before I go," he said.

"When and where did you say Velma's funeral is?" I asked. "I really want to pay my respects."

He hesitated a long moment, then said, "There are no concrete plans that I know of. Her body was just released today and the family is scrambling to find the money for a proper funeral."

He shot me a pointed look. "That's where you come in. Your generous offer might allow them to bury Velma with some sense of dignity."

"And by family you mean her son?" I asked.

He nodded.

"Please let him know that I really want to pay my respects so I'd appreciate it if they let me know when and where her service is." I pulled out a card and my checkbook. "What was her son's name?"

"You can just make the check out to *The Velma Harris Estate*," Shawn said, looking at some point over my left shoulder.

Hinky.

Everything about Shawn, SP Hawkins, Esquire felt off. I couldn't imagine why an attorney for someone would be this cagey with information.

"Make the check out to the estate? No. That's too cold. I'd really like to make it out to her son," I insisted. "I want him to know how very sorry I am."

"He's a client as well, and I'm not sure he wants me to name him," Shawn said slowly.

"He'd be named in Velma's obituary. And I'm not sure that his name would fall under attorney client privilege," I said. "You and I both know that even conversations between an attorney and clients aren't always protected."

Shawn Esquire gave me a look.

I smiled. "Didn't I mention that before I was a potter, I was an attorney."

Shawn was a pale man to begin with. And I could certainly sympathize. I'd occasionally joked that I was neon. The moment the sun hit my skin, it turned red. Neon or red. There was no middle ground for my complexion.

"You're an attorney?" Shawn asked, taking a rather large gulp of his Guinness.

I nodded, as if I didn't realize he was upset by the fact. "Yes. That's why I asked about your practice. Erie is a small town. I've probably heard of it, even if I don't know you."

That was a lie. Even when I was working as an attorney, I hadn't really spent much time circulating in legal circles. My father had been more than capable of that. Oh, I went to a couple local functions every year, but I avoided what I could.

I watched Shawn's face. He seemed surprised, then almost angry. "I still would feel more comfortable if you made the check out to Velma's estate."

"And I am paying this money as a way of apologizing to the family—her son—for the pain and trauma his mother experienced because of a fall at my store. I want it to be personal."

"Let me call and ask him then," Shawn said.

He took another long sip as he thumbed through presumable contacts on his phone. He finally hit one and put the phone up to his ear.

Trisha brought my salad and said, "Does your friend want anything?"

"I'll ask when he's done," I said.

She walked back toward the other side of the bar, but gave me a small nod, which I interpreted as she'd taken some pictures.

Shawn took another sip as he waited. Finally he hung up. "He's not picking up."

"No problem." I closed up my checkbook and put it back in my pocket. "Why don't you get in touch with him and then let me know so I can personalize the card. Or I can simply wait for the funeral and take it to him myself."

Shawn Esquire didn't seem to like that answer. "I..."

I could tell he wanted to argue, but he couldn't think of an argument. He picked up his glass, drained the contents and said, "I'll be in touch."

"Sure. Just let me know," I said nonchalantly.

Shawn got up and walked out of the bar. Without even offering to pay for his beer. He'd just left it for me to pick up.

That was annoying.

It wasn't about being a gentleman, it was about paying your own way. I would never presume that anyone was picking up my tab.

I was still fuming over his rudeness moments later, when Trisha walked down to my seat. "I snapped a number of pictures, in case some don't turn out. Who was he?"

"I'm not sure," I admitted. I glanced at the door he'd just exited. "There's something off about him. He's supposedly an attorney, though I've never heard of him."

She picked up her phone and her fingers flew. Moments later my phone pinged. "Thanks."

"You're not getting into trouble again, right?" she asked slowly.

"Trisha, would I do that?" I asked as innocently as I could muster.

She laughed. "Yes. But try not to. I'm looking forward to my classes in the new year. If you're incarcerated for interfering with a police investigation, I'll miss out." She paused and said jokingly, "Yes, it's all about me."

"Like I said, this was a police-sanctioned meeting." That wasn't quite true, but it was close enough. "I'll behave. I promise." I held up a couple fingers as if giving an oath of honor. Then I changed the subject.

I poured dressing on my salad and Trisha laughed.

"We do have other items on the menu," she said with a grin.

"But when you find something you like, you should stick to it."

"Says the lawyer who turned potter," she said, laughing.

"Touché," I said.

She reached for Shawn's glass. "Wait. Don't. Could you bring me a plastic bag and add the cost of a glass to my tab?"

She gave me a look that said she knew I was getting in trouble, but did as I asked.

After I bagged the glass and slipped it in my purse, I sipped my beer and tried to decide what I'd learned.

On the surface, not much. Velma had a son who shared an attorney with her.

That son didn't have enough money to pay for a funeral.

Something was off about their attorney. I had to confess, after reading the papers he'd sent me, I realized that he'd either got some online legal degree or not even that much. My first year professors would have laughed me out of class if I'd written such a jumbled mess.

I'd thought about asking Shawn about other claims, but since he wouldn't open up about a client's name without permission, I couldn't imagine he'd breach attorney client privilege.

Round and round and round.

I wasn't getting anywhere.

I ate my salad, finished my beer, thanked Trisha for the help and headed home. Lily came down the stairs to greet me. I let her outside and then went into my work area and stared at my idea board. I sent Shawn's picture to the printer and hung him up next to Velma.

I called Coco to see if she'd found anything on Shawn Hawkins, Esquire as I stared at the board.

"Hey, I don't have anything. I can find no record of an attorney named Shawn Hawkins anywhere in the States."

"How about Velma?" I asked.

"I've found more Velma Harrises than I anticipated, but none who match the description of yours. I have found a few mentions of a Velma Harris in papers. Some of those match your Velma though."

"From?" I asked.

"I can't prove anything yet, but I'm pretty sure your Velma was in New York and Massachusetts. I can't find any records of her living anywhere. No properties in her name. It's just her name that pops up in a few cases."

"What kind of cases?" Yes, I asked the question, but I was pretty sure I knew the answer.

"No arrests or anything. Just an article in a paper here, or an online blog there. Some slip and falls, but other small time scams, too. I'm still digging," Coco promised. "I can email you the links I have."

"And while I appreciate you're still digging, I don't have unlimited funds."

"I know that," she said. "You're my dig-into-it-when-I-have-a-few-extra-minutes case. I'll confess, even if you told me to stop now, I wouldn't. I'm intrigued. It's not often I find a ghost in this day and age. People have social media accounts and there's always a paper trail. Not with your Velma."

This tracked with my theory that Velma had tried to stay off the radar. "Thanks, Coco."

"Don't thank me yet. I haven't found anything official on Velma or her attorney."

"I do have a picture of him now, if that helps."

"Should I ask how you got it?" she asked. She sounded as suspicious as Trisha had.

I laughed. "I got it in a police-sanctioned way."

Okay, maybe that was stretching things a little. But Micci helped me write the letter, and I did call her when Shawn Esquire called me. I couldn't help it she didn't pick up.

Coco sighed. "I'm a good enough investigator to know you're hiding something, but yes. Send me the picture."

"Will do as soon as we hang up." Maybe this would help. If I could find out more about Shawn, maybe I'd find out more about Velma.

"Great," Coco said. "I'll send you links to the Velma mentions I've found. And Harry, don't worry about the bill. Seriously, I'm intrigued. Most of the background I dig up is easy and accessible. This isn't that."

"When things slow down, I was wondering if you could show me some of your tricks for digging up that kind of online information on someone." Not that I was planning to have future incidents with people who needed investigated, but it still sounded like a good idea to learn something.

"Sure. Maybe we'll work out a trade."

"How's that?" I asked.

"I'll take a class in exchange for what I'm doing and showing you the ropes on this kind of research."

I didn't hesitate, I just said, "Deal. Although I didn't know you had some overwhelming drive to learn ceramics."

"I didn't, but I'll confess, in the last few weeks your studio seems far more interesting than I'd imagined it could be." She laughed and I joined in.

"Wasn't there an old curse about living in interesting times?" I asked.

"I believe there was," Coco agreed.

I knew Coco in a cursory way through my father's firm. She wasn't a traditional investigator. She wasn't a classic gumshoe.

She was a data collector.

If you gave her a name, DOB, picture...she could put together a paper trail.

But not for Velma and her attorney. What did it mean?

I decided to load the kiln.

Why?

Because it needed done and because loading a kiln was like a puzzle. All those pieces had to be put into place in order to load it in the most efficient way.

I found it soothing.

As I leaned into the kiln and put the smallest pieces on the bottom shelf, I stood up and saw my kiln goddess on the shelf over the kiln.

One of the first assignments my ceramic professor had given was making a kiln god. I'd jokingly scoffed and said was I making a kiln *goddess*.

My professor was a good sport and laughed as well and assured me I could make a goddess.

She was less than expertly made, but still, after all these years, I loved her. She had beehive kiln for her body, flowers in her hair and a row of pots at her feet.

My kiln goddess was a story that would need to go in the book. That idea of finding your own path in art. The idea of taking what people had done before you and twisting it and turning it into your own.

So themes. Balance. Finding your own artistic path. Building off what came before and making it your own.

I stopped loading the kiln, with just that bottom shelf loaded, and hurried out to my idea board. I wrote *Kiln Goddess* on a Post-It and stuck it on the board. I wrote *Artistic Path* on another. Then *balance*.

I thought that was my biggest theme. Balancing an artistic life with real life. Balance what came before with what your vision was.

I thought about balance as I finished loading the kiln. As I sat down in front of my idea board still mulling, I called Micah.

"Hey," he said.

I could hear his smile. He was happy to hear from me. That thought warmed me.

"What's up?" he asked. "It's kinda late for you."

I glanced at the time on my phone. "It is. I was just getting ready to head upstairs and wanted to say goodnight. I missed you."

"I miss you, too. I'm sorry—"

I cut him off. "I didn't call for an apology. You don't owe me one. I totally understand being immersed in work. This case is important to you."

He sighed. "They all are, but you're right, this one more than most."

"You take whatever time you need," I said. "I'm fine. I really just wanted to hear your voice and say goodnight."

"Tomorrow night. Let's go out and do dinner and—"

"Or..." I let the word trail a provocative amount of time.

"Or?" he asked.

"Tomorrow night, let's stay in, order pizza and just hang out. Maybe live on the wild side and take Lily for a walk?"

At the sound of her name, she sat up, thumped her tail twice, then collapsed back onto her dog bed as if that action exhausted her.

Micah was enthusiastic as he said, "That is the best idea I've heard all day."

"Go back to work. I'll see you tomorrow. L—" I cut myself off in shock. I'd almost said, *Love you.* Just a casual way of ending a call. But proclaiming your love shouldn't ever be casual. And I wasn't even sure that's what I felt for Micah.

I mean, I knew I felt something. But I wasn't sure that something was love. It was definitely like. Like a lot. But love?

No, I was definitely not ready for something like that just a bit over a month into meeting.

"Harry?" he said. "Is everything all right?"

I realized I'd been quiet too long. "Sorry. I'm more tired than I thought. Lights out," I said, as if that was the L word I'd been about to use before.

"Lights out sounds good for me, too. I'll see you tomorrow."

"I can't wait."

I hung up before I could say anything else stupid.

I wasn't a casual *Love you* sort of woman.

I was a standard *goodbye* or *see you tomorrow* kind of woman.

Of course, I wasn't a *fall into a relationship fierce and fast* sort of woman as well. And yet, here I was, in a relationship with a man I'd known less than two months.

It was a conundrum.

One I wasn't going to puzzle through any time soon.

I thought about heading upstairs, but instead finished loading the kiln. It was easier puzzling out how to fit each piece in than puzzling out why Micah broke all my normal rules.

Chapter Eight

"Feelings. They are at the heart of all art.
Love. Anger. Hope.
If a piece is devoid of feeling...it's not art."
~Harry's Pottery

The next morning, my phone rang at an ungodly hour.

I reached over to my nightstand and saw Micci's name.

"What the hell, Harry?" was her salutation.

"Micci, I called you first, but you didn't answer. I tried to call him back and cancel, but he didn't answer. What would you want me to do?"

"Not put yourself at risk," she muttered.

"I didn't. I met him in a public venue. I didn't commit to anything. I..."

I ran down last night's events. "It's all so weird, Micci. A client's name isn't generally hidden by attorney-client privilege. I can't imagine why Shawn would feel he had to keep it secret. But good news is, I had Trisha take some pictures. I'll text them to you. Maybe you can find out something more about him than I could."

"You aren't supposed to be trying to find out anything about him."

"Well, not me exactly. I had my dad's investigator try to find him listed in any state's bar association. She couldn't. I do have an explanation for why he has no address...he's staying in an RV."

"Harry—" she started, revving up for what I assumed was going to be another scolding.

"This isn't on me, it's on you. I called. You didn't pick up. Why didn't you pick up, Micci?"

I swear, I could almost hear her blushing.

I know, that doesn't make sense, but there it is. Micci Dana was dating. I'd place a bet on it. And she was embarrassed to admit it.

"Who is he?" I asked, trying to see if I was right.

"He who?" she asked.

I just waited.

I heard her sigh. "Just a guy. I went out on a date."

"Good for you. I'll send those pictures and I swear when he gets in contact with me, I'll call you immediately."

"Fine."

"Oh, and I have a glass with his fingerprints on it."

This time she laughed. "Harry, unlike the television shows, if I took the glass in and tried to run the fingerprints of someone who isn't suspected of anything other than being a bad lawyer with a limited paper trail, I'd be in trouble."

"Yeah. I get that."

"This isn't a television show, Harry. Figuring out who murdered Velma will take work. I do want to talk to this Shawn because you're right, everything about him feels off."

"When he calls again—and he wants that money so I'm sure he'll call again—I will let you know immediately."

"That will have to be good enough," she said as she hung up.

There was no way I was going to go back to sleep after that.

I made my coffee, grabbed it and made an early start of my day. I was very much aware of the fact I was going to see Micah tonight.

By that evening, I was a nervous wreck.

It was ridiculous.

I knew it was ridiculous.

I mean, it was just pizza with Micah. Maybe a walk with Lily Potter.

Been there. Done that.

And yet...there was something new in the mix. My feelings for Micah.

That wasn't true. They weren't exactly new. They'd been growing over the last few weeks. I refused to define them, despite my almost slip last night.

I didn't want to name them.

But the thought was there, just under the surface.

I thought about changing my clothes before he arrived, but in the end, I wore my work jeans, t-shirt and favorite plaid flannel shirt. I purposefully didn't mess with my ponytailed hair. I didn't put on make-up.

I was just me and I wouldn't pretend to be someone else.

But when Micah rang the doorbell, I did feel a spurt of happiness.

I opened the door and despite the fact I hadn't primped, I could feel my ridiculously huge smile as I saw him, pizza box in hand. "You're here."

"I am," he said. "Is that smile for me, or for the pizza?"

You. That's what I wanted to say, but instead I said, "Pizza of course. But I'm happy to see you, too." I kissed his cheek as casually as I could muster.

We walked up the stairs and Micah set the pizza box on the counter.

"I have a nice red," I said, pointing to the bottle on the counter.

"Sounds good." He went to the drawer and took out the...bottle opener? Cork puller? Wine bottle opener? Corkscrew.

It might have taken me a second to remember what to call it, but Micah knew just where it was stored. He was at home here. That thought warmed me.

He opened the bottle, got out the wine glasses and poured us each a glass.

He sniffed his glass, then took a sip. "That's nice."

"*This* is nice," I said, talking about being with him. The wine could have been grape juice for all I noticed. "I missed you."

There, I let him know that I felt something without being too specific. "I meant what I said last night, I get it. I don't miss you in a loud demanding way, but in a *I-notice-when-you're-not-here-and-I-feel-your-absence* sort of way."

He kissed my cheek and said, "That was the nicest thing anyone's said to me in a very long time."

"I—"

I cut myself off a moment. Trying to decide how to say what I wanted to say. I took a deep breath and decided to stop being a coward. "I haven't talked about my ex much. It's awkward to talk about an ex with someone you're getting to know. But I want to explain..."

I was making a muck of things.

"When he left me he said it was because he wasn't happy. He hated that I spent nights working at home. He wanted things to be all Alex all the time. I'm not wired that way. Even now that I'm not doing legal work, I take my work home with me."

Micah chuckled. "Both ceramics and mysteries."

"Yes. It wasn't until Alex said the words that I realized I wasn't happy in our marriage either. When I asked myself what would make me happy, the answer was this studio. And I was right...it makes me happy. So here I am. I didn't go looking for a new relationship. But you're here and I really miss you when you're not. You've become a part of the fabric of my life and I like that. I treasure that. When I said I missed you, that's what I was referring to. I feel your absence when you're gone. But..."

This was the important part of my soliloquy. "But I understand when you need to work. I understand when you just need a night to yourself. I think the fact we both have outside interests and jobs makes the time we are together better. I just wanted to make sure you understand that when I say I miss you, I'm not whining because you're busy with a case. I just notice that you're not here and feel your absence in a good way, if that makes sense."

I suspected it didn't make sense.

But Micah pushed his glasses back on his nose, as if he wanted to be sure he was seeing me clearly. And almost in slow motion he smiled. "I understand what you're saying and I agree. I like when you get that distracted look on your face because you're thinking about a project, or the book...or even a murder. I understand what you're saying. Both of us are adults with work we're passionate about. And that's okay. Because I miss you too when I'm not here. And while I'm pretty passionate about work, I'm also pretty passionate about you."

It was one of the most romantic things anyone ever said to me.

I didn't need to be the center of Micah's universe, but it was nice knowing I was part of it. And an important part of it.

At that point, we both forgot about the pizza and proceeded to show each other how important we were to each other.

A long time later, we finally ate our pizza.

It was cold, but hey, I liked cold pizza.

The next morning, I had another slice of cold pizza for breakfast with my coffee. Micah was sitting next to me, having the coffee but not the pizza.

"I don't know how you manage that," he said, eyeing my breakfast with disdain.

I laughed. "Cold pizza in the morning tastes exactly the same as cold pizza at night." I paused. "What I'm saying is, it tastes good."

He shook his head and sipped his coffee. "Want to get together for dinner tonight?"

"I'd like that. I know your case starts Monday, and next week will be crazy for you. I was thinking about what we talked about last night and I will be using it as a code."

"A code?" he asked.

"When I text you, *I miss you*, it means *you are part of my life, and I understand what you're doing is important. Missing you has no guilt or expectations attached to it. I want you to know that I feel your absence and look forward to a cold pizza reunion.*"

He smiled. "That's a lot for three little words, but let me just say ditto."

He left for work and Lily and I went down to the studio. Adi showed up a half hour later. She gave me a look and said, "What are you so happy about?"

"Life. Just life in general," I said. You know that point in a Disney movie where the heroine thinks life is perfect? Birds are singing...and generally so is she? Yeah, that moment. That's how I felt at this moment.

"Would life in general have anything to do with a certain attorney?" Adi teased.

Even I knew that my smile was absurdly large, but I couldn't help it. "Maybe," I admitted.

She chuckled and reached in her bag and handed me a sheet of paper filled with drawings. "This is from Nori. She said she knew you'd miss her today, but her grandma needed some lovin' too. She said she'll be back next week and wants to make a red-tailed hawk."

"A hawk?" I asked.

"She checked a book out of the library."

We chatted a few more minutes about Nori's raptor passion, about Micah and I even brought up Barnabas, which made Adi blush. "We've been spending a lot of time together," she confessed.

That made sense because I hadn't seen much of my friend lately. "Why don't we all try to do dinner together one night? We haven't done a neighborhood gathering in a while. Miss Betty's been at her daughter's but she's supposed to come home this weekend. Maybe we can do a welcome home party next week?"

"That sounds wonderful."

I promised I'd set something up then I retreated to my studio and Adi got ready in the shop.

I'll confess, I loved Saturdays. With Adi here, I could work in peace and quiet. I stared at my Idea Board as I wedged clay.

I didn't look at Velma's side. No, I swiped right and looked at the book ideas. My goal was to put this all together and send an outline and opening to the publisher by February 1st.

Goals.

I put that on a Post-It and added it to the wall. I made goals all the time. They kept me on track and kept me moving forward. That was especially important in a job where I was my own boss.

Goals and...

I was poised to write a second note when I heard the front door open, loud voices, and then my studio door open all in the space of time it took me to set the pen down and look up.

Christine Patterson, from CrisP's Deli, stood at the door between the shop and the studio.

Adi came running up and said, "Harry, I'm sorry. I told her—"

"It's okay, Adi. Chris, come in and have a seat." I motioned to one of the long tables I used for classes.

She shook her head. "I'll stand thank you." She vibrated with annoyance...maybe anger?

For the life of me, I couldn't think of what I'd done to annoy her.

She took a deep breath. "I want to say, I didn't do it. I heard you're looking around at people that Velma woman scammed and the fact you haven't come to see me yet means you think I'm a suspect, but I'm not. I have a temper. Yes. And she put a business I've worked myself to the bone to build at risk. So yes. I might have yelled at her and been pissy, but that doesn't mean I murdered her."

Chris's deli was a wonderful place to grab lunch. Adi and I didn't eat out often, but on occasion on days she worked, we'd order in a sub or a quart of soup. Chris made the best soup. "Chris, I never said or thought—"

She interrupted. "Sure you did. You talked to Adrienne and Cindi. And who knows who else. But you haven't come by the deli have you? That Velma woman was a scam artist. And she was just mean. Her lawyer was a jerk, too. And now that I've said that if he dies, you'll probably think it was me, too. Right? You'll talk to your cop buddy and I'll be hauled in. Well, I didn't kill Velma and I wouldn't kill her stupid lawyer. You can tell your detective buddy that. I paid her that three thousand in cash and I'd have enjoyed kicking her cane out from under her if I were that kind of person, but I'm not. And I'm not the kind who would kill her either."

"I didn't know she scammed you, too," I said softly.

That took the wind out of Chris's sail. "What?"

"I just started putting out feelers, hoping to talk to others who were scammed by Velma, but your name hadn't come up."

"I thought..." She glanced at my idea board. I hadn't had time to cover it up before she came in. She came closer, studying it. "I'm not up there."

"No, you're not," I agreed.

She took a deep breath. "I'm sorry. I know you went to Chili Pepper's and she's new to the downtown, so you hardly know her. I kept waiting for you to come to my place and when you didn't I figured it was because you were gathering more intel on me. I didn't do it," she added as if I might have missed that part.

"Can I get you something to drink?" I asked, hoping to help her calm down. "Why don't you grab a chair and tell me about your experience with Velma Harris. I think the best thing all of us can do is come clean about what happened. Eventually something will show up—a pattern, a piece of information—and we'll know who it was."

She sank into a chair and I got her an iced tea.

She took it, took a long sip and said, "I'll tell you what I know."

And she did. It was the same story I'd heard before, though Velma did buy things at

Chris's. She had a fondness for ChrisP's soups. "She always bought our wedding soup. I teased her once and said she was going to be as strong as Popeye the way she ate it. She scowled and said she hated spinach. That she had to eat around it because I didn't make it right. She was a mean old lady."

At least she bought things from Chris. She'd never bought so much as a spoon rest from me.

"So now what?" Chris asked.

"It's going to be okay," I said. "I'm going to give you the detective's number and you'll call her and let her know everything you just told me. Do you know anyone else she scammed?"

"Just Steve," Chris said.

"Steve?" I asked.

"Steve Leslie. From Calico. He's the manager."

Calico Saloon was historic themed. The staff dressed as sailors, farmers, and pioneers. Erie's local hero, Oliver Hazard Perry occasionally tended bar, along with George Washington, who technically visited neighboring Waterford.

It was more a tourist restaurant than one for locals.

But if Steve simply managed the place, that didn't quite fit the bill. Owners of small businesses have a stake in them. A manager didn't. They were just employees.

"He was so angry," Chris said. "As if Velma's fish bone was somehow his fault. I tried to assure him he wasn't the only one. I told him that they were better off just paying her and putting it behind them."

I wasn't sure this was the best advice, but didn't say so. "Was the owner angry?"

"The owner is Steve's uncle. He doesn't care what Steve does with the place as long as he gets his checks in a timely fashion," she said.

"Looks like I'm going to Calico next week. I'll talk to him and see if he'll call the detective, too."

Granted, I could just tell Micci and let her handle things, but I'll confess, I was curious.

I knew the pieces were there, but it was tough to see how they all fit together.

And I wanted to see how they all fit together.

"Calico's hours are cut way back in the winter. Just Fridays, Saturdays, and Sundays," she said.

That made sense. Erie's tourism had grown, and though I thought Erie was particularly lovely in the winter, we didn't get nearly as many visitors during the snowy season. "Then I'll go tomorrow after brunch at my dad's."

"Okay, call your detective and let's get this over with."

"You can call her yourself," I said.

"I'm too nervous. You call her and then I'll talk to her."

So I called Micci who set up an interview with Chris on Monday. I assured Chris it would all be all right. I asked if she wanted me to come with her. "No. I think I can manage it, but if I feel like I'm really a suspect will you come and represent me."

"Yes," I promised.

After Chris left, I thought I'd finally get some quiet. I just wanted to sit and throw something simple and think. I wedged a dozen balls of clay, put them in a bag.

There were a few people in the shop, so I started throwing a cup. One of the reasons I put glass between the studio and shop was to keep the dust in the studio. Ceramics is very dusty work. It was a very fine dust. I worked hard to keep the studio spic and span, and I followed best practices for keeping the dust at bay, but there was no way to avoid it all together.

Keeping the spaces separate made sense.

But the other reason I put the big window in is that people really seem to enjoy watching the process.

So I nodded at the customers out there and started.

Center. Drop a hole. Pull a wall. Finish.

Set that one aside to dry and start another.

I sank into the rhythm. Losing myself in the process.

Halfway through my balls of clay, I heard a tapping on the window. I looked up and saw Phyllis. I smiled and waved her in.

She didn't smile back.

As she opened the door, I could see just how upset she was.

I wiped my hands on a towel and stood up. "What's wrong? Is it Dad?"

She shook her head and gave a small hiccup. "Oh, Harry, I'm sorry. No, he's fine."

"Let's go upstairs and talk," I said. Having customers watch me make pottery was one thing, having them watch my almost-stepmother break down was another.

Phyllis followed me up the stairs. Lily was on our heels. She'd become such a shadow that I'd have been surprised if she hadn't followed us.

Lily flopped on her upstairs' dog bed and I got Phyllis a glass of water and said, "Tell me what happened."

"It's Dylan. He's been..." She shrugged. "I know you've never seen him at his best. You've seen him moody and non-communicative, but that's not him. Dylan is—was—funny and normally smiling and all that started to change a couple years ago. He pulled away from me. I thought he was just finding his own path and needed to break away from me. For so many years it was just the two of us. Even in his teens, we got along. But the last couple months have been worse. I don't know if he resents your dad. I don't know if he's in trouble. He won't say so I don't know what's going on with him. I've tried everything. I thought maybe you'd see what you could find out. I mean, I know you're not a working detective, but you have a way of looking at the world and putting things together. Your father is proud of it. I thought maybe you'd see what you could find. Maybe it's me and your father? Maybe he resents me getting married again after all these years?"

The second time she said that made me realize this was her greatest fear. That somehow her happiness with my dad was going to alienate her son.

How could a mother make a decision like that?

I might not have known my mom for long enough, but I knew then just as I knew now she loved me without reservation.

Phyllis started to cry, as if having to decide between her son and my father might break her.

I was no detective. Even now with Velma, I was more collecting information and passing it on than *detecting*.

Still, seeing Phyllis's pain, I couldn't help but say, "I'll talk to him. Almost-big sister to almost little-brother."

"Really?" Phyllis said.

"Really. I'll..." I tried to come up with an excuse to get together with him. "I'll tell him that I want us to do something for you and Dad. Something special to celebrate your wedding."

Phyllis reached out and took my hand. "Harry, I don't know how to tell you how much this means to me."

"I don't want anything ruining your day. You and Dad deserve nothing but happiness. I'll talk to him." I might be new to this big sister business and I might be older than Dylan, but I was closer to his age than his mom. I was a neutral party. Hopefully I could reach him.

Phyllis left me with his contact information and filled in a bit. Dylan was a computer programmer who'd graduated from college last year. He had a job and she said he liked it well enough but his true love was computer gaming. He'd been in competitions and made some money at gaming. I didn't know that was a thing, which made me feel decidedly old.

"Dylan was a change of life baby. I didn't think I'd ever have a child and then there I was, halfway to old and pregnant. My boyfriend wanted nothing to do with a kid and left, but I didn't mind. It was always just me and Dylan. Whatever's happening, I'll do what I can to fix it. I miss my son," she said.

I hugged her. "I don't know what I can do, but I'll try to help."

"Thank you, dear. Like I said, I never thought I'd have children, but first there was Dylan and now there's you. I'm so very lucky."

And for someone who hadn't had a mother in decades, I felt a warm glow settle over me as I said, "I think I'm the lucky one, Phyllis."

I lost my mom when I was nine. I knew that Phyllis would never replace her, but I was old enough to realize Phyllis didn't need to. She'd found a space in my heart that was all her own. It took nothing away from my mother and only made my life richer.

After she left, I picked up the phone and called my almost-little-brother. "Dylan, it's

Harry. We have to talk. What are you doing this afternoon?"

"Why?" he asked. I couldn't decide if he was being snappish or just suspicious.

I opted to believe the best of him and said, "I want to do something for the wedding. I was hoping you'd help."

I had no idea what I wanted to do, other than talk to him. But he agreed and I let out a sigh of relieve.

I went down to see Adi. "I have a family thing," I started. It sounded weird. I'd only ever had Dad and he wasn't high on drama. "Would you mind if I left at two? Could you close up?"

"Sure. What's up?" she said.

"A new brother." I didn't know anything about dealing with siblings. Nothing about being an attorney or being a potter prepared me for anything like that.

"Brothers. They are not for the faint of heart," she said, sounding wise and knowledgeable.

Adi rarely spoke about her family and I didn't pry. But since she brought it up, I asked, "How many?"

"Three. Three older brothers."

"Oy," I said.

She nodded sagely. "Oy is right."

At a few minutes after two, I was sitting in a booth at *Down by the Bay*. It felt weird. Micah and I always sat at the bar. But whatever was up with my new brother, I thought a booth was a better option.

I thought meeting somewhere neutral was the best option and frankly, the bar was starting to feel like a second home to me.

Dylan didn't scowl at me when he came in, but he didn't smile either. He looked wary.

"Dylan, I'm so glad you could come," I said, nodding at the seat across from me.

He slipped in and got right to the point. "What's this about Mom and your father?"

"Would you like something to drink?" I asked.

He shook his head.

I took a sip of my iced tea and rather than beat around the bush I said, "First I hoped you and I could come up with something to give our parents for a wedding gift. I am making them mugs but I wanted something special from the two of us."

"That was first, what's second?" he asked.

"Your mom is worried about you." There. No beating around the bush at all. "She came to see me because she's so worried. She cried, Dylan. I may not have known your mom that long, but she's truly been nothing but awesome to me. And she's always so happy and upbeat. Seeing her cry..." I just shook my head.

He froze. "She cried? She's worried?"

"Listen, you don't know me from Adam, but we're going to be family. You're going to be stuck with me from now on. Family occasions, brunches, holidays... And I don't think either of us has a lot of experience with family. I've had just Dad and you've had just your mom, but I have friends who have bigger families and I know they can be messy and loud and crazy...and maybe sometimes a little pushy. So I'm starting out our sibling relationship by being pushy. Your mom's worried there's something wrong. She thinks you might be in trouble and it's killing her that you won't let her help. She said you used to be one of the happiest people she knew. Frankly, that was a surprise to me. You seemed sullen when we met and nothing since then has changed my opinion. But like I said, if there's something wrong and you don't want your mom to know, maybe I can help."

"Why?" he asked.

"Like I said, we're family. I'm the big sister you probably never wanted, but also, like I said, I have friends and know that even when they think they don't want their family, families can be handy. I don't have many uses. I've got a law degree and know how to make stuff in clay. And I'll help you with either of those if you need it. But I also have a good shoulder and I'm willing to lend it to you if it'll help."

He sighed and something in him loosened. "I've been a pill. I know it. It's just that I saw you and Micah all coupley and Mom and your dad. I was pissed that I couldn't be that. Not mad at you or your dad, or even my mom. At me. At myself."

"Why?" I asked.

He looked uncomfortable.

164

"I'm pushy and also an amateur detective too, so you might as well tell me."

He gave me a half smile. "I've always suspected, but now I'm out of the house and I've known since college for sure. I'm gay."

I felt genuinely confused. I just couldn't imagine that would be a problem for Phyllis and I knew it wasn't for me or Dad. "And?"

"And my mother doesn't know," he said slowly.

I tried to imagine it was me. No, I'd never come out to my dad. But I remembered going into his office to tell him I was going to quit being an attorney and quit his practice to be a potter.

That had been hard.

He hadn't had a clue how unhappy I was. And he wasn't happy that I was quitting. I remember the sting of his disappointment.

And I remembered back in college telling him I wanted to be an art major and study pottery as a career path.

That had been hard and hadn't led to anything since he browbeat me into pursuing law.

No, that wasn't fair. My father hadn't done anything to me. I did that to me. I could have stood up to him. I could have insisted. It took Alex leaving for me to find the strength to pursue what I wanted.

First I said the words that needed to be said, "Thank you for sharing that part of yourself with me."

I wish I'd read up on how to handle this. I hadn't, so I just followed my heart. "I imagine it's scary, not knowing how your truth will be accepted. I know what's it's like admitting something important about yourself to your parent. Not on this level," I said softly. "But Dylan, I honestly think your mom can handle it."

"I've tried telling her. But she's always teased me about someday being a grandmother. I don't know how to take that away from her."

"First, how old are you?" I asked.

"Twenty-three."

It seemed like forever since I'd been that young. Oh, I occasionally still got carded, so I wasn't quite a crone yet, but I felt much older than my new little brother. "That's a long time to hold onto a secret like that. And secondly, you can still be a father. There are options."

"I know, but..." He trailed off.

"Families are messy, but they support each other. I've got your back. No matter what, I'll stand by you."

"Since she has you checking up on me, maybe you could mention it to her? Sort of ease her into it."

I snorted. "Nope."

"What if she looks at me in a different way?" he asked.

I could tell that was his biggest fear.

"I suspect she will," I admitted. "For the first time you'll be the real Dylan, not just the Dylan you think she wants you to be. That will definitely shape the way she looks at you. For the better I think. But if what you're asking is what if she rejects you? Then you and I will get up and walk out together. You've got a big sister now. I'll have your back," I said again. "And I know how hard it is telling a parent you're not who they thought."

He shot me a look that said he wasn't buying it.

"My dad thought I was an attorney. And I was working as an attorney, but in my heart that's never who I was. It wasn't until I was in my thirties that I had the strength to tell him I was a potter."

"It's not quite the same," he said with a small smile.

"Maybe not, or maybe it's more the same than you think. Every parent has an inner-view of who their child is. It might shake them to find out that view is all wrong. But Dad and I are good now, and I suspect you and your mom will be as well. You tell them whenever you're ready. And whenever you're ready, I'll have your back."

I didn't know what else I could do or say to make this easier for him. I'd waited a long time to tell my father who I really was and what I really wanted. Dylan could take as long as he needed and I'd be there for him.

My big sister duties done, I said, "Now about a gift. I have an idea."

Half an hour later, we were back at the studio, laughing as we crafted our parents' gift.

Micah came over at six with a bag of groceries. "Do you have enough in those bags to feed my little brother, too?" I asked.

Dylan smiled at me.

I could see Micah wondering what was going on, but he just grinned and said, "There's always enough for one more."

"Oh, you're in for a treat," I said to Dylan. "You should know your big sister can't cook, but Micah? If he stops lawyering, he'd have a new career in chefing."

And Dylan smiled at that. At that moment I truly understood what Phyllis had been missing. That smile.

"Do you think I should practice on Micah?" Dylan asked.

"Practice what?" Micah asked.

I saw Dylan look at me before he took a long breath and said, "I'm gay."

"Nice. Are you dating anyone?" Micah asked as if Dylan's proclamation was no big deal. "Because if not, there's this guy I know—"

"Oh, no, Dylan. Micah's inner-yenta is showing. So tell me about this guy you think might be appropriate for my brother," I said.

We all laughed. And I could definitely see just what Phyllis had missed. I nudged my new brother as we both teased Micah about playing matchmaker.

It was a good night.

Chapter Nine

*"Sometimes the simplest object can turn into
something amazing and beautiful."*
~Harry's Pottery

Although I was confident my father and Phyllis would handle Dylan's announcement supportively, I was still on pins and needles for him. I wasn't sure if he'd tell them at brunch today or not.

Either way, I supported him. Whenever and wherever.

I remember how nervous I was when I told my father I was quitting. I think every parent's child is torn. They want to make their parents proud by living up to their expectations and yet, they want to be true to themselves. Frequently those two things don't align.

I sat next to Micah and Dylan sat across from us. I could see his anxiety. It was almost palpable.

I nodded, hoping it gave him some encouragement.

As Phyllis placed a roast in the center of the table and sat down, Dylan cleared his throat, took a long, deep breath and said, "Mom and Josiah, I have something to tell you."

The table stilled and Micah took my hand in his.

Dylan took another deep breath, looked at me and said, "I'm gay."

I waited for their reaction, but they still wore puzzled expressions.

"That's it," I said, trying to help him out.

Phyllis walked over to his seat, hugged him "Than you for telling me."

She went back to her own seat, as if nothing monumental had just happened.

From Dylan's expression I knew he was shocked. "I'm sorry to shock you."

"Dylan, I'm not shocked. I love you. I love who you are and who you are growing into. And I'm glad you shared this piece of yourself with me. I have always and will always love you. There's nothing you can do or say to change that. There's no one you can love who will change that."

That was it.

I could see that as Dylan realized what had just happened, he relaxed.

Maybe it was anticlimactic. But Phyllis had spoken the truth and anyone could see it. She loved Dylan.

My dad finally said, "Be true to yourself, Dylan. The rest of the world can either accept you or well, screw 'em."

I was pretty sure I gaped at my father. The language was one thing, but the sentiment was another. He winked at me as if to say it had taken him a while to learn that lesson, but he had indeed learned it.

"Is there someone in your life, Dylan," Phyllis asked.

"Bring him to dinner some time," my dad added.

"No one dinner worthy just yet," Dylan responded.

He looked at me and shot me a true, bone deep smile. And at that moment, I truly understood what Phyllis had been missing in her son. I smiled back and the moment was over. Talk turned to the wedding.

I said, "Dad and Phyllis, what do you need from us for next Saturday?"

"Less than a week. I can't even believe it," Phyllis said. "But it's such a small ceremony. I don't think there's anything to worry about. We have champagne and I ordered a cake. That's about it."

My father cleared his throat. "That's not it. Ask her."

Now it was Phyllis's turn to look nervous. "I was hoping you'd consider being my bridesmaid. I mean, I know it's ridiculous. This is just a small, intimate no fuss wedding, but we will need someone to witness the marriage certificate and—

I cut her off. "I'd be honored."

My father nodded in such a way that I knew he'd been sure of my answer. Then he asked, "And Dylan, I'd be honored if you'd stand with me."

There it was, that smile again. Dylan nodded at my father. "Yes, sir. I'd be happy to, sir."

Everyone's nerves seemed to settle down after that. We ate, talked about the wedding and just...well, just did family stuff. I had brought champagne and we all toasted each other.

I know there are people who take a family brunch for granted but not me. After years of quiet meals with Dad, I was going to revel in all these moments.

Every single one.

When the meal ended, I said, "Dylan and I are going to do the dishes. We have a lot of sibling bonding to make up for. So while we do them, we will definitely complain the entire time about how our parents aren't fair. And maybe for good measure, we'll argue over who you two love the most."

Dad and Phyllis laughed as I shooed them out of the dining room.

Micah shot me a look, asking if I wanted him to stay and help. I shook my head and he shot me one of his knee-weakening smiles before he followed Dad and Phyllis into the living room.

"Are you okay?" I asked Dylan as we stacked dishes and carried them into the kitchen.

"I am. I feel like for the first time, I can just be me. Like, if I met someone, I could invite him to brunch and no one would care." He filled the sink with water.

"Oh, don't be *too* sure about that," I warned with a smile. "We'd all definitely care and grill him like he was on the witness stand, trying to be sure he was good enough for you.

Dad will be super blunt about it, but I promise I'll try to be more subtle."

Without discussing it, Dylan started washing the dishes and I started drying them, as if we were siblings and had done this hundreds of times.

Dylan paused and said, "I wasn't sure how I felt about Mom and your dad. I think I was a bit selfish, wishing things wouldn't change, but I think this whole family thing might be kind of nice."

I felt exactly the same way. "I've never been a big sister, but I promise to do my best to torture you and support you in turn."

He laughed and said, "And I swear to do all those little brother things that all big sisters hate." At which point, he finger-flicked water at me.

I called out, "Hey Phyllis and Dad, Dylan's flicking water." Then I stage whispered, "Tattling is definitely a big sister thing."

I heard the laughter in Phyllis's voice as she called out, "Don't make me come in there, you two."

"If your mother's threats don't work, just know I'll be right behind her," my staid and buttoned up father teased.

Dylan and I collapsed in laughter.

This.

How I missed this growing up. For a moment I wondered what it would have been like if my mother had lived. Would I have had a sibling? And if I did, would we have been best friends?

I liked to think we would have been. I liked to think my mother and I would have been best friends as well. We'd have girls' days out. Lunches. Shopping.

Okay, I hated shopping, but I did like to eat. We'd chat about this and that. She give me advice.

Yeah, I was pretty sure my mother and I would have been close.

And I thought that Phyllis and I would be. Not that I saw her as a replacement for my mom, but as a new and lovely addition to my family.

After the holidays and her wedding, I'd make it a point to do more with her.

Dylan and I served the lemon chiffon pie in the living room and then did those plates up as well.

As we finished he said, "Really, thank you for everything, Harry."

"We're family now, Dylan. And though I don't have a ton of experience, I've heard this is what family does."

As Micah and I left, Phyllis hugged me. Not just a social ladies-hugging sort of thing, but a true bear hug sort of thing. "Thank you. I don't know how you did it, but thank you. Dylan hasn't seemed so carefree in years."

We left Dad's and walked toward our cars.

"Do you have time this afternoon?" Micah asked. "I know next week's going to be nuts for me, so I thought we could spend the day together, if you can."

"I would love to spend the afternoon with you. Any chance you want to go to Calico's for dinner?"

"Isn't that a touristy place?" he asked. And he gave me that lawerly look saying he knew there was more to this than dinner.

"It's a place where families go to have a good time and good food for a good price," I tried.

He snorted. "You're switching careers again and going into advertising?" he asked.

"No, I think I've found another Velma target," I said.

He sighed. "Of course you have. Let me guess, they work at Calico?"

"He manages it," I said.

"So dinner and a show?" he said.

I kissed his cheek. "Yes. But in the meantime, maybe we should go home and relax after that brunch. And by relax, I mean take a nap. And by take a nap, I mean…" I whispered exactly what I meant in his ear.

It turns out, a nap sounded very good to Micah too.

And by nap, I mean we got absolutely no sleep at all.

Calico's was a medium size restaurant with a stage that stood above the dining room.

They had a frequently-changing rotation of short, five to ten-minute musical skits they put on every hour. Tonight's theme was *Christmas in Erie*. The supposed kids in the skits asked Santa for Christmas presents reflecting their era. Most of it was set to music. It was as corny as it sounded, but actually pretty fun.

The wait-staff and kitchen-staff were the actors.

Most of the show was generic enough that out-of-towners would enjoy it, but some of it was very Erie-centric. For instance, when a kid in the sixties asks to meet Santa "under the clock" it was a shout out to our premier downtown store at the time, *The Boston Store*. The building and clock were still there. I think most Erieites had visited, or at least knew of it.

This was no Broadway musical and the lead singer was no Audra McDonald, but it was cute. I found myself laughing out loud at a few of the lines. When they finished their ten-minute skit, the crowd clapped enthusiastically.

When our waiter came back—he played a young Oliver Hazard Perry—I said, "That was marvelous."

He smiled. "Thanks. We have a lot of fun."

"By any chance is Mr. Leslie around tonight?" I asked.

He laughed. "He's always here. This is his baby."

"I'm Harry Lawe and I own a pottery studio—"

He interrupted and grinned as he said, *"Harry's Pottery*. I have one of your mugs. I used it for coffee every morning if it's clean."

"Thank you. It always means so much to hear people use my work. I was wondering if Mr. Leslie had a moment if he could stop by so I can introduce myself."

Young Oliver nodded. "I'll let him know you're here."

"You do know you're a potter not a detective, right?" Micah asked.

I laughed. "Yes. And this isn't like last time. I'm turning everything over to Micci. I just have a chance to talk to people as one small business owner to another. That's something she can't do."

That was part of it. Knowing that Velma had tried to extort money from me was another part. And finally there was the puzzle aspect of things. I really just wanted to figure it out.

"You're like a dog with a bone," he said. "But I do appreciate you're not getting hauled down to the police office as often this time as last time."

I snorted. "Knock on wood."

He reached out and rapped the table just as a jovial looking man approached our table. "You must be Harry. I'm Steve. And you are?"

"Micah McCain. A local attorney." He nodded to the chair and Steve took the seat.

"Harry, I've meant to stop by your shop," he said. "I've heard wonderful things about it. I saw the mugs you did for *Down by the Bay*. I thought maybe we could discuss something for *Calicos?*"

"That would be wonderful," I said. "Stop by any time. I'll give you the grand tour. The show was adorable."

"Thank you. I wrote it. I write them all." I could see his pride in the show.

"You write them all?" I asked.

"Yes. My wife said I run the restaurant in order to get to pretend to be a playwright. I know it's not Broadway, but I love it."

I nodded. "I believe in following your passions. I was an attorney before I was a potter."

Steve whistled. "That's some change."

I laughed. "Yeah, that's what my father said." I paused a moment and said, "I know you don't know me, but I heard you might have had a run-in with V—"

That's all I needed, just that first letter.

His happy expression faded. "I'd spit if I weren't in a restaurant. I don't want to get some health code violation. But that woman was a menace. I know I shouldn't speak ill of the dead, but she was awful."

"She slipped and fell at my place," I said slowly. "She wanted me to pay her off."

He grimaced. "She ordered fish tacos here and claimed I tried to kill her with a fish bone. And fish happens," even in the midst of his anger, he amused himself, "but she acted so...well, fishy. I was pretty sure something was up. And when her lawyer called the next day—"

"Shawn Hawkins?" I asked.

"Yes. He called the next day and said we could make her pending lawsuit against me disappear with a small cash payout. He asked for three thousand dollars. I said I had to ask the owner about any cash expenditure over a thousand. He gamed it out but ultimately took a thousand. I knew I should fight it, but who has the time for a lawsuit? I didn't want to get a reputation here in town. And I didn't want to get my insurance involved. It seemed like the easiest way to go, but now, I hear she did this kind of thing all over town and I feel embarrassed I didn't fight. As if I let the entire DBA down. I'm not a man who usually cowers in some corner."

"I hear you. I'm and attorney and I didn't want to get in some legal fight with her." That wasn't quite the truth. I'd been itching to take Velma into court, but I had the knowledge and could have fought for years without it costing me more than my time. I understood why non-attorneys made their decisions to just settle.

"I signed a nondisclosure, so I didn't talk, but that was a problem, too. We all should have been talking. I've got to think now that she's dead she can't enforce the clause. Right?" he asked.

"I think she'd be hard pressed to. I think everyone feels that way because a lot of people are starting to talk." I got out Micci's card. "This is the detective who's overseeing the investigation. You should probably give her a call."

"Am I suspect?" he asked.

"I don't think you're any more a suspect than the rest of us downtown business owners are. It's about helping the detective fill in the blanks. What Velma did and whom she did it too. It shows a pattern. And somewhere in that pattern is a clue about who murdered her." I thought of my Idea Board. I'd put up Steve's name and a thousand dollars.

"It could have been just random. It could have been an accident," he said.

"Yes. It could have been. But..." She was shot. If she'd been hit by a car or found in the lake, I'd have thought there was a chance it was an accident. I was no detective, but it seems to me getting shot in her home was pretty up close and personal way to kill someone.

Did the gun mean it was premeditated? Someone planned to kill her and brought it along? Or was it there? Was it Velma's, or did the killer just carry a weapon all the time.

But why shoot an old lady?

Because they were angry. Sure.

I was angry.

Adi didn't own the studio but she was angry.

Everyone Velma scammed was angry.

But to be mad enough to kill someone, that was a completely different kind of angry. A much darker, twisted anger.

"I'm no detective," I said, ignoring Micah's quirked eyebrows at my statement. "I'm just a part of the community and hear things that a detective doesn't. So I'm just passing her information about the other business owners who were scammed."

"So you're like a junior detective?" Steve joked.

"Maybe a detective's assistant?" Micah who'd been quiet, letting me handle things, said.

"I'm a potter. Maybe a writer someday. But not a detective," I told them both.

"She likes puzzles," Micah said to Steve.

Steve started singing. "She's a puzzle solving, potter who finds bodies in her kiln. A junior detective who will find out who's killin' it. The wheel in her studio can't spin as quickly as her mind. She..." he paused. I recognized the tune from *The Pirates of Penzance*.

"I'm stuck on the next line, but I'll figure it out."

"Please don't," I teased.

That made him laugh as he got up. "I'd better get back to work, but I'll call your detective. And hey, if Quincy Mac can be a maid and a detective, you can be a potter and detective. A clay spinning gumshoe solving a slip and fall. Isn't slip watery clay?" He cracked himself up.

I laughed. "Like I said, I'm happy enough with just being a potter."

"A potter who likes puzzles," Micah said, still laughing at Steve's song.

Steve was humming as he left.

I looked at my comic boyfriend. "Maybe Steve will let you help with the next show?" I said.

"Maybe. Everyone knows that attorneys are wannabe novelists. And he has a good start with that song."

I chose to ignore the song and said, "Everyone knows attorneys want to be novelists?"

"Sure. Maybe not just novelists. Maybe books on pottery, too." He grinned.

I couldn't help it, I laughed.

"I want to say thank you though," he said.

"For what?" I asked.

"For including me. For not feeling as if you have to hide this curious part of yourself from me. I know I was joking when I said you like puzzles, but you do. I saw how happy you were about your holiday jigsaw puzzle."

"I haven't touched it in days, but I'll get back to it. It's a tradition. Mom loved doing jigsaw puzzles. She got one out every year. That first year without her, it hurt so much, but doing a puzzle helped."

"That's a lovely legacy. But for you it's more than just an annual jigsaw puzzle. Your idea board is really your puzzle wall. You have an idea of something you want to make and you mull it over, puzzle it through and figure out how to make what's in your head come out in clay."

I'd never thought about it like that, but maybe he was right.

"I think that's why you liked contracts. They're really just big puzzles. Seeing how everything fits together in a way that's best for your client."

"This doesn't sound like some random insight," I said.

"I've been thinking about you. You see, I like puzzles, too. And you, Harry Lawe are a giant puzzle. One I very much want to figure out."

I laughed. "Everyone is a bit of a puzzle."

"True."

"So tell me a piece of your puzzle I don't know," I said.

He thought a moment. "My sister's coming in town for the holiday."

"I don't know if that qualifies as a piece of your puzzle," I said.

"You're wrong. Our families are definitely a part of our individual puzzles. Beyond that, Millie is just puzzling." He grinned at his sister-dig.

"I can't wait to meet her...unless I'm being too presumptuous." That was the thing with my relationship with Micah. On one hand, I felt so close to him. On the other hand, things were still new. It was a weird place to be.

He snorted. "I'm glad you can't wait to meet her because she's coming here under the guise of spending Christmas with me. Mom and Dad are going on a cruise, so we're both on our own. That's what she says. But..."

"But?" I asked.

"She wants to check you out. And by check you out, I mean interrogate you with a tenacity that only an attorney could truly admire. Unless that attorney was the one on the receiving end."

"Uh oh," I said.

I remembered my first visit to Micah's. He'd offered up Millie's bath bombs. Back then, which seemed so long ago but wasn't, I'd wondered if this Millie was a girlfriend. Or an ex-girlfriend. Now I knew. And she was coming to Erie to check me out.

"Millie's going to love you," Micah assured me, but there was something in his voice that made me wonder if she would. "The question is, will you love her? Millie can be an...acquired taste."

Miss Betty came home on Monday and I took her to the grocery store to stock back up. "We'll get back to our normal schedule next week," I said.

"I missed you. I love my daughter, but this is my home. I missed the neighborhood."

"I have an idea," I said.

I made calls. We had a makeshift welcome home dinner. Barnabas brought his mother, Mama Lonnie. Her cooking was right up there with Micah's. And he brought Adi. Hap and Kitty Meyers jumped at the invitation. I invited Trisha, too. This had been her house and these had been her neighbors. I provided pizza.

"Hey, Lady Bug," Barnabas said as he came and sat next to me on the couch. He took up a lot more space than I did. "How're you doing?"

"Good," I said. I didn't have to ask how Barnabas was doing. He was practically glowing.

"Where's Micah?" he asked.

"He started a new trial today. I don't think I'll see much of him this week." The thought reminded me again how much a part of my life Micah had become. The thought should be terrifying to me, but it wasn't.

"But everything's good?" my friend pressed.

I thought about what I almost blurted out the other day and nodded. "It is." I could feel my cheeks heat up.

Obviously, Barnabas noticed because he laughed. "Good. I like that boy."

"What boy do you like?" Mama Lonnie asked, as she joined us.

Hap pulled up two chairs and settled Kitty and Miss Betty in them. "What are we talking about?" Miss Betty asked as Hap brought two more chairs. One for him and one for Trisha.

"A boy Harry likes," Mama Lonnie said.

"Micah," Miss Betty said knowingly.

"That lawyer boy?" Miss Lonnie asked. "You two are a couple now?"

"We're..." I searched for a description. "Dating."

That seemed like a lackluster description, but it was accurate enough.

Adi came out of the bathroom with Nori, who settled herself at the counter with a stack of paper and crayons before she joined us. "We're talking about Harry and Micah. It's one of my favorite subjects."

I looked at her. "You have thin walls," she said to me then turned to my friends and neighbors and said, "I've known they were going to be a thing since the first time I saw them together."

Barnabas hummed the tune from *Sitting in a Tree* song we'd sung in our school days.

I shot them both a look. "So maybe we should all start discussing who likes who and…"

I saw their expressions and stopped. They might be happy to discuss me and Micah, but they weren't ready to talk about whatever was going on with them. They didn't look like they'd appreciate being teased and I didn't want to throw a kink into something so new and tenuous. So I dropped it.

"How was your visit with your daughter, Miss Betty?" I asked, trying to change the subject.

I wish I hadn't asked when my sweet older neighbor's face darkened.

"She said maybe it was time to think about going into a home, as if I am too old to take care of myself. I changed that girl's diapers and held her hand when her heart got broken. I took care of her. I've never asked her to take care of me. I don't appreciate her trying to tell me what to do."

She stopped and laughed. "Maybe I am getting older, but I've been lucky to have such good friends to help me out. Don't think I don't know how much you all do for me."

"Miss Betty, you know we're here to help you not because we have to, but because you're one of us. You're the heart of this neighborhood," I said and everyone else murmured their agreement.

I was one of the newer members of this community, but they'd made me one of their own. They gave me a sense of belonging. And I knew after my *unfortunate incident*, they all would have my back no matter what. That was such a rare and wonderful thing.

"To the neighborhood," I said, raising my beer.

Everyone else followed suit and repeated, "To the neighborhood."

It was a nice night. I felt fortunate to live in a neighborhood. A real, help-each-other-out sort of neighborhood.

Trisha might not live here anymore, but she was still a neighbor. Everyone had welcomed her back.

It was a lovely evening.

The only thing that marred the night was how much I missed Micah.

After everyone left and I cleaned up the mess, I texted him. *I miss you.*

I miss you, too.

I might not be saying the three words I'd almost said before, but what I said was enough. For now.

Chapter Ten

"I think that people love stories about things like **The Unfortunate Incident** *because it makes us feel less alone. Everyone has lived through their own version of an unfortunate incident, so everyone can relate to the story and connect. I meant what I said to Mr. Leslie, his skits are art. I think that's what art is... seeing or hearing something that makes us feel a little less alone."*
~Phyllis Lawe, quoted in
Harry's Pottery

Tuesday night, I talked to Micah. The trial was going well. He thought they'd wrap things up in the next couple days, then it would be up to the jury.

"We'll celebrate when it's over," I said. I was truly amazed by how much I wanted to see him. He'd become part of the fabric of my life. By the calendar it had happened quickly, but it didn't feel quick. It felt as if he'd always been a part of my life.

"I feel pretty confident we're going to win this, but you never can tell," he said.

"Either way—win or lose—we'll *celebrate*." I put just the right emphasis on the word celebrate.

Micah laughed, which had been my intent. "I do miss you. Maybe I should come over—"

"Nope," I said. Someone had to be strict around here. "Do your prep for tomorrow than go to bed."

"I can go to bed as easily at your place," he said with more than a hint of suggestion.

I chuckled. "Let me clarify. Go to bed and sleep. You know that's not what we'd be doing here."

"I really do miss you."

"I miss you, too. Call me tomorrow when you can." Not strings. Not demands. Keeping it light.

That's what I told myself. But how I felt about Micah was definitely feeling more than a little stringy.

"I'll call," he promised. "I..." He hesitated a long time before he said, "I'll talk to you then."

After we hung up, I thought about that pause.

I...

I...

I...

I like you?

I miss you?

I wish we were celebrating?

What had he thought about saying?

What did I wish he'd said? I was pretty sure that was the more pertinent question. What did I want Micah to say to me?

The questions and possibilities tumbled round and round in my head. I needed a distraction.

I was deciding if I should do more work, read, or watch a movie when my phone rang again.

I smiled. "Just go to bed already," I teased.

"Harry?" said a voice I recognized. A voice that wasn't Micah's.

My mood decidedly dropped as I realized who it was.

"Shawn. Sorry. I thought you were someone else," I said. "What can I do for you?"

"I talked to Velma's son. I can come over and fill you in," he offered.

No way did I want to be alone with Shawn Esquire at eight p.m. in my empty shop. There was no way to have Micci just chillaxing discreetly here.

"How about the bar. In an hour?" I said. I was very much a homebody. If I were going to be anywhere at nine p.m., it would be in my studio or out with Micah. Catching up with a creepy, questionable attorney wasn't something I wanted to do, but I wanted to know about Velma's son, who until now had wanted to remain anonymous.

"Bring your checkbook," he said then hung up.

I called Micci.

"Micci, it's Harry."

She sighed an unbelievably long sigh. "Harry what did you do now?"

"Shawn wants to meet again. He said Velma's son okayed him talking about him and to bring my checkbook. He wanted to meet here—"

"I hope you said no," she said.

"Of course I did. I said we'd meet at the bar again. That will give you a better chance of being unnoticed there. I'm so detectivey."

"Harry," she said, her voice sharper than normal. "You are a potter. A potter who is providing me, the key investigator, information. It's every citizen's duty to help the police. When you're done tonight, you'll go back to throwing clay and I'll go back to throwing the bad guys in jail."

"Yeah, Micci, you don't sound all that intimidating when you call them bad guys," I said. "Perps. That sounds better."

"For the record, I don't need to sound intimidating, because I *am* intimidating."

"Tomato, potato," I said.

"That's not how the saying goes," Micci, still very much the cop, informed me.

I laughed. "I know. I used to say it that way when I was younger and it stuck." I had a sudden vision of my mother, laughing as I said it. I was pretty sure that's why it stuck. It reminded me of her.

"Let's be clear on how this is going to work. You'll wait, meet Shawn and see what he wants. I'll stay in the background until you're done then I'll talk to him."

"I'll see you soon."

I let Lily out and she curled up on the couch as I got ready to go. "I'll be back soon girl," I said.

She was already snoring.

Sleeping is what Lily did best. She was the perfect studio dog.

I left and headed down to *Down by the Bay*. It was really cold tonight. The clouds that normally blanketed Erie in the winter had given way to a clear sky. The stars were bright and the moon was full.

Tonight I'd get some answers.

No, Micci would get some answers, I corrected myself.

I might be playing amateur sleuth like Erie's own Quincy Mac on occasion, but the real role I wanted to play was potter.

Things were going well at the studio.

I wanted to put Velma and her invisible son and Shawn, Esquire behind me and concentrate on the book. They were all useless distractions for me.

Distractions.

Now, that was a good subject in the book.

Any creative endeavor could be sidetracked by distractions.

For some potters that was family and kids.

No kids here yet for me, but certainly there was plenty going on with family and friends to distract me.

I started to think about all the other ways people could get distracted.

And before I knew it, I was walking into *Down By the Bay*.

"Harry," Trisha called out as I came in.

A guy I'd seen more than once at the bar nodded at me. "Hey, where's your fella?" he asked.

You know you're a regular when people at the bar recognize you. I smiled. "Busy tonight, but I'm sure he'll be down again soon."

"Good. You two seem like a nice couple. I wouldn't want to hear you broke up." He smiled.

I smiled back. "Nope. We're still good."

"Good."

I walked down toward my normal seat and tried not to be annoyed to find someone was in it.

It's not as if I owned it or anything.

Habits.

I was a creature of habits. Pottery was a one of my habits...the rhythm of my life. And that was a good thing, but getting stuck in a rut was not.

I took a closer seat at the bar and Trisha brought me a beer.

Yes, routines and habits were good things and conversely bad things.

Having a bartender who knew your drink was a good thing.

This was definitely a theme for the book.

I grabbed a napkin and wrote *distractions, habits and routines* down, then scribbled a few more notes.

"Harry?" Shawn said as he sat in the seat next to me.

"Shawn." I nodded at the empty seat.

He snapped his fingers imperiously at Trisha as he sat down. "I'll have a coffee."

"Sure thing," she said. When she was out of his view she made a face at me and I totally sympathized.

"So, I talked to Velma's son and he's forgoing a service for his mother. He's simply having her body shipped home to West Virginia and buried there," Shawn said.

I tried to be ambiguous as possible. "I see."

Shawn nodded. "And he did give me permission to give you his name."

Trisha came and set his coffee down. "Thank you," he said without bothering to look up.

The fact he had to get permission to give me Velma's son's name was just another oddity in this case. I couldn't think of too many reasons why an attorney would hide a client's name. This case was so weird.

Thinking about Shawn as part of my case hit me. Not my case, I reminded myself.

This was Micci's case.

"He said you can make the check out to Paul Harris."

Weird. It was just weird.

"Like I said, I'd rather give the check to Paul personally," I maintained.

Shawn sighed as if I were truly the most difficult person he'd ever met. "And as I said, Paul values his anonymity. He didn't get along well with Velma."

I decided I was done play Sally Do-Gooder. I just shook my head and said, "Listen, that's fine. This was just me trying to do a nice gesture for him. I felt bad about his mother falling at my place, though I never felt guilty about it. She was old and in fragile health. If he didn't get along with her and didn't care for her, then maybe he's not suffering her loss. In which case, while I still feel bad about Ms. Harris, I don't feel as bad about Paul. Please simply send him my condolences."

I drank the rest of my beer and started to stand.

Shawn said, "No, wait, wait, wait. I didn't mean to imply this hasn't bothered Paul. It's his mother after all. Losing her is worse because they never had a chance to heal their relationship. He's going to go through the rest of his life knowing he didn't have the kind of relationship he wanted with her and knowing there's nothing he can do about that. It's tragic."

"I so understand that. I lost my mother when I was young and all these years later, I not only missed her but I missed the kind of relationship we might have had. I'd have called her up and asked her to come for coffee, or called her for help making my first holiday meal, or have her there at my wedding, or the birth of my kids..."

I stopped because I was legit making myself feel bad.

I thought about Phyllis and realized that though she'd never take the place of my mom, I thought we could form a special relationship. I could imagine her helping me with a holiday meal…

Shawn interrupted my thoughts. "Yes. That's it. So you see."

"I do," I admitted.

"And?" he prompted.

"Listen, this is just so weird. Velma's son's in hiding. I get private, and I get mourning a relationship that never got to develop. But I don't get you here now instead of him. I don't. And I don't get why you, Velma's attorney, are part of this whole weird situation."

I stood again as if I were going to leave.

Shawn Esquire's face turned beet red as he stood facing me. "Listen, Paul deserves that money. His mother fell at your establishment."

"Not because of some fault of mine," I informed him. "I took pictures to ensure that if this went any further, I could prove that. No water. No dust. No cracks. She fell either because she was prone to falls or because something was wrong with her or because she was a scam artist."

"How dare you?" he asked.

"Listen, I'm done, Shawn." I put money on the bar for Trisha. "Tell Paul I'm sorry for his loss and wish him well." I walked to the door and gave Micci a nod as I went by her.

I turned as I opened it and saw her approach Shawn Hawkins, Esquire and say, "Mr. Hawkins. I was hoping you would come down to the station and answer a few questions."

At that moment, Shawn looked at me with such palpable anger in his eyes I shuddered.

I hurried out the door and didn't hear the rest of their conversation. But as I walked past the window, I saw Shawn was still looking at me and glaring.

He was not a fan.

Oh, well. I wasn't a fan of Velma's hinky lawyer either.

I was officially done with this nonsense. I'd hooked Micci up with various leads and I'd connected her with Shawn. She was right—she was a detective and I was a potter. I was happy to leave it at that.

I walked home and pushed thoughts of Shawn and Velma out of my mind. Instead, I thought about my mom and Phyllis.

I went in, then back out again to walk Lily. It was cold enough she didn't press to go far. She was a dog who valued comfort. We got back inside and she curled up on her dog bed.

"You're like a Hobbit," I said with affection.

Then I called my almost-stepmother. "Phyllis, what are you doing Friday night?"

"Harry, dear, what can I do for you? Did you need something?"

"It's not what I need. As your bridesmaid it's my duty to take you out to celebrate. You need a bachelorette party."

"Oh, Harry, that's sweet, but I don't know that I'm up for anything too raucous. I—"

"Micah and I just went to Calico's. They're only open weekends in the winter, but they put on a very cute dinner show."

"That sounds perfect dear. Just perfect."

"Is there anyone you'd like me to invite?"

"I have some friends, but since I'm not inviting them to the wedding, it would be awkward to invite them out the night before. So if you don't mind hanging out with just me, the two of us would be fine."

"Phyllis, I truly love hanging out with just you," I assured her. Then we chatted a while and I felt bad I hadn't planned something sooner. I truly didn't want Phyllis to fill in as some sort of surrogate mother, but she was family. And I wanted to let her know that I was happy about that.

Calico's it was.

Micah called. "The case went to the jury this afternoon. I'm hoping we hear back tomorrow."

"That's good. I've missed you."

"Me, too."

I told him about Shawn and Phyllis. "We're going out on Friday night. It's not really much of a bachelorette party, but I wanted to do something."

"Maybe I'll take your dad out," he said.

"And ask Dylan?" I prompted.

"Definitely." He paused a moment then said, "Millie's going to be here Sunday. Want to come over for dinner? I'd like it if you two met."

"You've got me halfway scared of your sister, but yes."

"You're going to love her," he said and after a dramatic paused added, "Eventually."

"And how is she going to feel about me?"

"The same. Millie's an acquired taste. But she's also one of the most generous people I've ever met."

Generous sounded nice, but acquired-taste not so much. "You're not making this better," I told him.

"So dinner tomorrow, then Friday with your dad and Phyllis respectively, then the wedding, then Millie," Micah said.

I hummed the theme from *Jaws*.

"I might have exaggerated. It won't be that bad. She's really great."

I suspected it wouldn't be that good either.

"Night," I said eventually.

"See you tomorrow."

"I missed you," I said before I hung up.

The next day, Micci still hadn't called me.

I get that. She was the detective and I wasn't even an amateur sleuth on this one. No Quincy Mac-ing it for me. I was just a gatherer-of-some-intel.

Yeah.

I was more a spy than detective.

Harry the Spy.

There was a book, *Harriet the Spy*. Yeah, with a name like Harriet, I notice when it's used.

So Micci wasn't going to pass any information on to me. Fine.

I tried to tell myself it didn't matter. I wasn't Micci's partner. But I still felt bad. I'd been very open and forthcoming this time round and maybe I thought that meant she'd reciprocate.

I tried to forget all about Micci and Velma and Shawn and Velma's invisible son, Paul.

My part in this was over.

I'd put a curtain over my idea board so I could hide my dead-body-kiln investigation notes from visitors to my studio. This time, I pulled the curtain over Velma's half of the idea board because I was done with that. I left just my book ideas out.

The book side was filled with themes, ideas, chapter titles...

Maybe it was time to start writing the proposal and actually outlining what I was thinking.

I brought my laptop downstairs. I rarely brought it into the studio because of the pervasive dust, but I wasn't claying today...I was writing about clay.

I fell into the process just like I used to fall into writing a contract. I found a certain satisfaction in creating order out of the chaos of my Idea Wall.

I wrote the word *Balance* at the top of the page as a reminder.

I started with an actual school type outline. I listed Chapters. Subheadings. Short bursts of facts for each section.

I tried to balance each part with tangible information and intangible thoughts. I could teach anyone how to create something out of clay. That was physical. Tangible. But art...that was something else entirely. I saw the spark in some of my students. They had an inner-vision and a drive to turn something ephemeral into something with form.

Those sparks of artistry were why I opened my studio for classes. Hoping that in each class I'd find someone with passion. Someone with that spark.

I worked and thought.

I typed and stared blankly at my Idea Board.

I deleted and added and rearranged and mulled.

I took short breaks whenever customers came into the store. I had thought things might slow down, but they kept up a steady pace, even though Christmas was less than a week away.

I'd long since finished my gifts. Except for Micah's. But his would be done in time.

Every time I got up to wait on someone, I worried I might lose my flow, but I didn't. Those breaks brought me back to the outline with renewed enthusiasm.

It was a good work day. A day when I was just a potter looking at my art from a new perspective.

Ten minutes before I planned to turn the open sign to closed, a half dozen women walked in together.

One of them said, "I know, I know, we're here late. We promise we'll be quick and we'll make it worth your while even if we run a bit past your closing hours."

"Dorthey, you're awful. Do you mind?" another woman asked me.

"No, please. Feel free. If you stay late enough, I won't have to cook."

"Really?" another lady said.

"My boyfriend's coming over and he's a much better cook. So if I'm trapped here with customers, he'll take pity on me and at least help with dinner."

The woman laughed. "Of course, you can't close up on customers. A savvy small business owner understands that. Plus you'd never close on friends. Let me introduce us. Dorthey, Linda, Joanne, Susan, Jeannette and I'm Margie. And you're Harry, so we're not just customers, we're friends."

"Ladies, it's so nice to have *friends* supporting the shop," I said. "Can I help you with anything specific or do you just want to browse?"

"We'll browse," Margie said.

"Speak for yourself, Margie. I'd like to ask how you're doing after last month's…" Susan hesitated.

It was sweet that she did. Most people hadn't been that polite.

"*Unfortunate incident*," I filled in. "That's how I've chosen to refer to it. And thank you, I'm doing fine. Is that how you heard about the shop?"

"No," Linda said—the introductions had gone quickly, but I thought it was Linda. "I brought the girls here because I love pottery. I've got a small collection from Pigeon Forge and local potter, Tom Hubert. I've thought about taking a class someday."

"Whenever you're ready, we offer classes here. I have a Friday night *Wine and Mud* group, but it's filled to the brim so I'm starting a few more classes after the new year. If you leave your name and email, I'll put you on the mailing list."

I pushed a sign-up form toward her and noticed how many more names there were since last time I looked. Adi must have been busy.

"Oh, that's perfect," maybe-Linda said.

I watched as she signed. Definitely Linda.

The ladies made their purchases...more than enough to make up for staying open a bit late. Just as I was bagging the last one, Micah walked in.

"Is this him?" Dorthey asked.

"Him who?" Micah asked, grinning at the group.

I'm pretty sure a few of them swooned.

"Him...the boyfriend who cooks," Margie said.

I felt myself blush as she called him my boyfriend, even though it was accurate. I still wasn't accustomed to hearing the word bandied about.

Micah didn't seem the least bit embarrassed. He pushed his glasses up higher on his nose and grinned. "I am the *him* in question."

Margie gave me a bold wink. "A man who cooks is a keeper."

All six ladies gathered their packages and called out holiday greetings as they left.

"Late night?" Micah asked, glancing at the clock.

I turned the sign to closed and locked the door.

"Not too late for this..." I walked into his arms and hugged him. "I have missed you."

"Ditto," he said.

"So tell me about the trial," I said.

"How about I tell you while I cook you dinner?" Micah asked.

I thought about Margie's proclamation. She was right, but I felt obligated to say, "I can cook," without being too forceful about the offer.

He laughed. "I know. But I like to cook and you don't."

I nodded. "There is that." I double checked that the door was locked, turned off light and then followed Micah up the back stairs to my apartment.

Micah did cook dinner...eventually.

But first we showed each other how much we missed each other.

Turns out we missed each other a lot.

Micah left at six the next morning. "I've got to run home and get showered and changed for court. We're expecting the jury to come back today."

"See you tonight then to celebrate?" I asked.

He smiled. "Definitely."

"And Micah, I know this is a small apartment, but I suspect I could find enough room for you to hang a suit...if you want. No pressure. I mean..."

He stopped me with a kiss. "Yes. Just to be clear, I already cleared out a drawer and some space in the closet for next time we were at my house. I planned to make the same offer."

I laughed. Not that it was funny, but because I felt bubbly.

This.

Micah and I were on the same wavelength about so many things. Everything about the two of us felt right.

We hadn't been together that long, but I was starting to forget what my life was like before he was a part of it.

He started for the door. "Oh, hey, I meant to ask about Velma. You said something about Shawn. Anything new?"

"I'll tell you all about it tonight. But I'm pretty sure Micci's got this and doesn't need my help." I still felt a bit disappointed by that, though I understood. Well, mostly understood.

He kissed me again. "I feel better. Tell me tonight."

"When we celebrate," I said.

"Fingers crossed."

He left and I drank the coffee he'd made. There was something endearing about a man wearing yesterday's suit crossing his fingers.

Thursday was a repeat of Wednesday.

I had enough customers that I didn't bother trying to work with clay. Instead I kept plugging away at the book proposal.

I felt better and better about it.

I hadn't been sure how I felt about trying to write a book, but the more I worked, the more I was convinced this was something I'd enjoy.

I never minded writing as an attorney, but it had been rather cut and dry.

This? This was freedom.

It let me write about things that I—as a potter—would want to read about.

Not just the how-to, though I was suggesting some of that. But it was the creative part of art I was excited about.

Why I created.

The idea of taking something that existed only in my head and turning into a physical presence was one of the most rewarding things I'd ever done. I'd left security for—

Halfway through that thought, a repeat customer came in. "Miss Georgia, how are you?" I asked as I hurried into the shop.

"I'm fine Harry. I'm looking for something for my pastor. She's a single lady who always seems a bit disheveled, but she's got a giant heart and no family to speak of. I want to be sure she has something under the tree Christmas morning. Last week she talked about going to Williamsburg and watching the craftspeople there create. *Creation* was the theme of her sermon."

I liked that her theme corresponded with what I'd just been thinking.

"Wait, I have just the thing." I led Georgia back to the area I kept an assortment of mugs. Some were sets, but many were just one-offs.

"Here," I said, picking up the one I'd been thinking of. It was part of my "Bee" collection.

A small raised bee with a series of Bee phrases under them.

"*Bee* Creative," she read. "Oh, Harry it's perfect. I always love coming in here because you always have just what I want even when I'm not sure what I want."

After I rang her out, she pulled out a small brown bag. "Now, this isn't a present. I was just at a house-sale and they had this wonderful assortment of weird kitchen items and I've seen some of what you do with texture and I thought of you. There are these spiky wheel things. I was thinking they're for pastry, but I'm not sure. Maybe they're for something sewing related. I thought they might be something you'd think was fun."

I opened the bag and it was a cornucopia of fun. There were pronged wheels...pie crusts? A large pick sort of thing. Maybe an old ice pick? I picked up a flat textured plastic thing. "I'm not sure what this is, but oh, it might make a cool pattern."

She grinned. "I'm so glad you like them. I see how often you use texture in your pottery. I still use my tree-mug every day it's clean."

I knew what she was referring to. I'd done a series of mugs where I'd carved the bottoms out to look like tree bark. Some had smooth handles, some carved ones. I loved those mugs, but they weren't really great moneymakers. They took a lot of time, and it was hard to recoup that from customers. I only made a few for the shop and the rest were for me.

"I'm so glad you like it. And I'd really like to pay you for these."

"Harry, it was a house-sale. The last day. 50% off everything. I think that entire bag cost me a couple bucks. You can consider it a tip for all the times you've had exactly what I needed. And I will keep an eye out for other fun looking tools. Don't ever feel as if you have to use them, but they might be useful sometime."

"Thank you, Georgia," I said. "These really are great."

This. This was what had been missing in my law career...a chance to really connect with people. "Seriously, thank you."

"Merry Christmas, Harry. You had a heck of the year. Here's hoping next year is much more peaceful," she said.

"I don't think I could handle a second year like this one," I said with a laugh. "Merry Christmas to you, too, Georgia."

When she left, I admired the tools spread out on my counter. They would be handy.

I locked the door, switched the sign to *Closed* and went back to my Idea Board. I added a Post-It that said, *People.*

Then I went back to the computer and quickly wrote:

Art is about connections and creation. When I make a piece, there's an intent behind it. Something I'm trying to artistically capture. Even if it's the plainest of bowls. There can be beauty and intent in that simplicity.

But when someone buys a piece, or I give them a piece of my pottery, my intent ceases to matter. Theirs is what matters. What they see and feel when they use that piece is what matters.

I think of my pottery as a craft because art seems like a pretentious word. But this once, let's say art. There's a give and take involved in any art. What the artist intends and what the viewer experiences.

I made a piece, Dyad Emerging. For me it was about the act of transformation. Of leaving something behind to become something else. I wonder if the person who bought the piece sees that in it or sees something else entirely.

I thought those paragraphs were a beginning to a chapter on *Creation*. I'd have to tell Georgia and her minister that they'd inspired me. I glanced at the clock and knew I was done for the day.

I hurried upstairs to change for my night out with Phyllis.

Two hours later, I sat across from Phyllis at *Calicos*.

"This is wonderful," Phyllis said as she clapped as the skit ended. "This was so kind of you, Harry. Who knew that building the Millcreek Mall could be such a cute little musical?"

Yes. Steve had been at his creative best with that little skit about our local mall.

"Not me," I assured her. I would never have imagined a mall's history being turned into a musical, but it was kind of cute. "So do you need anything for tomorrow?"

I suspected my father had dated a few women when I was younger, but I'd never met any of them. I'd asked him why once and he said, "*When I meet someone I plan to bring into our family, you'll meet her. Not until then. Who I date shouldn't worry you at all.*"

And it hadn't.

If he'd asked, I might have pointed out that I was an adult and could handle the fact he dated women who weren't my mother. But he'd never asked and I never said.

That pretty much summed up our relationship until recently.

Until Phyllis.

"Really, I'm happy to do anything to make the day easier for you."

"No, dear. We've really planned such a small, simple ceremony. We just wanted our kids, a few close friends to be with us. The cake and champagne's at the house. There's nothing much to do but say I-do. And Harry, I do. Thank you for accepting me. You've been so sweet and welcoming. I love Dylan, but I always wanted a daughter. I know I'm not your mother, but I'm glad we're carving out a relationship."

I reached across the table and patted her hand. "I feel so lucky."

"So Harry, who do we have here?" Steve Leslie asked as he approached our table.

"My..."

How to introduce Phyllis? My stepmother? My father's fiancée?

I settled for, "My friend and family, Phyllis."

"Oh, that's perfect," he said in such a gleeful I knew I wanted to see Steve play Santa Claus in whatever holiday production he did. All he needed was a Ho Ho Ho to fill in the picture.

"We're trying out a new skit tonight and I hope you both enjoy it." He pulled up a chair and sat down. "We've been holding onto it for your next visit, Harry. When I saw you here, the cast got ready."

As if on cue, all the staff disappeared and our waitress reappeared in the middle of the stage wearing an artist's beret and holding a large, ceramic bowl.

An artist's life is crazy.
Security can be hazy.
I do love my pottery and glazes
I don't love bodies pushing up daisies
My name is Harry.
Dead bodies are scary...

And then Harry burst into a song about finding that first body and soon, one of the bartenders joined in wearing Harry Potter-esque glasses and singing about protecting me, or rather the waitress Harry...

Ten minutes later, waitress Harry had solved the mystery and was kissing her attorney.

The curtain closed and the '*cast*' came back onto the floor and went back to their jobs.

"What do you think?" Steve asked.

I was speechless. I didn't know what to say.

But Phyllis saved me. "It was marvelous, Mr. Leslie. I am loving how you take Erie history and current events and turn them into art."

"Art?" he said as he blushed.

"Yes, art," Phyllis repeated. "Art is the ability to look at the world and show a reflection of what you see to others. Harry does that with her pottery and you do it with your skits. It's impressive and I loved it."

He literally puffed out his chest. "Thank you ma'am. That means a lot. Harry?"

I wanted to say I wasn't fond of having the worst moment of my life portrayed as a comedy. But I paused a moment and thought about classic pratfalls. I suspect the person falling never thinks it's funny, even though the audience does. That's right, my life was a pratfall and I couldn't fault Steve for seeing the humor in it. So I diplomatically said, "I never imagined my life warranted becoming a musical, but you really captured my *unfortunate incident* in just ten minutes."

He clapped his hands. "*The Unfortunate Incident.* That's the new official title of the skit."

He got up and headed toward the kitchen. "*The Unfortunate Incident,*" he bellowed.

"You hated it, didn't you," Phyllis said.

"Yes, I did," I admitted. "I never imagined my life would be entertainment for others. The way Steve presented it was comic and cute, but in actuality, when I was living through it, the experience was scary and crazy."

Phyllis reached across the table and patted my hand. "I think that people love comedy and things like *The Unfortunate Incident* because it makes us feel less alone. Everyone has lived through their own version of an unfortunate incident, so everyone can relate to the story and connect. I meant what I said to Mr. Leslie, his skits are art. I think that's what art is...seeing or hearing something that makes us feel a little less alone."

"Can I quote you in the book?" I asked.

She laughed. "I'm not sure it's an overly original or profound statement, but definitely."

"You're sure there's nothing I can do for tomorrow?" I asked.

"Just be there. That's all your father and I want. We want to be surrounded by our family and friends."

"That's easy enough. I'm so happy you're marrying him."

"I'm so thankful you've been so kind and accepting. I'll never be able to thank you enough for what you did for Dylan."

"We're family," I said. "I'm so excited about having a little brother. I think being a bossy older sister might suit me."

We both laughed as I paid our check and left.

Tomorrow was going to be a wonderful day.

Chapter Eleven

"Despite your best work and best intention, some things don't turn out like you planned."
~Harry's Pottery

I was walking on air after I dropped off Phyllis. Tomorrow was going to be a wonderful day. I was so happy for my dad and frankly, I was happy for me as well. I'm not sure I ever realized how much I wanted a bigger family until I found out I was getting one.

I opened the door and called Lily, then took her for a quick walk around the block. Quick because it was cold and the wind was blowing across the lake, making it feel even colder. Wind chill wasn't for the faint of heart.

"Brr," I said to the dog. Yeah, sometimes I talked to Lily. I would start to worry if she talked back.

I shut the door, double-checked that everything was locked up and walked up the stairs to my apartment. I flipped on the light and Lily started barking.

"You're finally home," said Shawn. "Shut the dog up or else."

There was a handgun visible on his lap.

When I was young, a neighbor, Mauri, hid in the apple tree in our neighbor's yard. When I walked by it on the way to school, she dropped out of the branches right in front of me. I screamed so loudly three neighbors came outside to see what happened.

My fright this time was worse than that, though I didn't scream.

In that split moment a jumble of thoughts raced through my mind. Could I make it down the stairs, unlock the front door and make it outside before Shawn could shoot me? I didn't think so. Could I scream loud enough for a neighbor or passerby to hear? Nope. Was there anything else I could do or exploit to get away from him? No.

Shawn patted a gun on his lap, silently reminding me of his threat.

"Lily," I said, grabbing her collar. "Let's go."

I dragged her into the bedroom and shut the door. Something I could exploit? I realized there was one thing. I dialed Micci's number on my phone, clicked the volume down in case she answered and stuffed it in my pocket. I wasn't sure if the mic was strong enough to pick up what was being said through a pocket, but it was my best bet to leave some kind of record if things went south.

The phone took a split second. I walked back out to my uninvited guest, determined not to let him see how terrified I was.

"What do you want, Shawn?" I asked, impressed that my voice held steady. I wanted to give Micci as many clues as I could. "Why would you break into my house with a gun?"

"I wanted money from you, but I didn't get that. I wanted you to stay out of the investigation, but I didn't get that. I wanted whole heck of a lot from you, but I didn't get any of it. What did I get?"

I was pretty sure it was a rhetorical question, so I didn't say anything. I wasn't sure I'd be able to stop my voice from quivering and I didn't want that.

"I came in through a basement window and then checked out your studio and saw your board with my face right in the center. How did you get that picture?" His anger was palpable.

Opting for the truth, I said, "A friend took it."

"Of course, normal people have friends. I've never had a friend. Did you know *that* with all your amateur detecting? Did you try to find one of my friends and talk to them? Because there are none. None. She took care of that, didn't she?"

"She?" I asked.

"Don't play coy. You know, don't you?"

I knew a few things and suspected a few more, but I didn't think I knew whatever it is he thought I knew. "Know what?"

"Pretending to be ignorant doesn't suit you. I looked up your law school records. I talked to people. I know that you know who I am."

I didn't say that what I knew was Shawn was Velma's lawyer and had dubious law credentials. I was pretty sure he meant something other than that. I was pretty sure I

218

was getting a fair idea what it was, so I just nodded.

He shifted in the chair and for a moment I thought he was going to raise the gun, but instead he reached in his back pocket and took out a five-dollar bill. "I'm hiring you as my attorney. So anything I say is confidential."

I shook my head, more convinced than ever he wasn't legit. "That's not how it works. I wouldn't work for you if I could. You represent Velma who threatened to sue me. That means my working for you would be a conflict of interest."

"It's not if I say it's not and she's dead, so there's no conflict. I'm hiring you and you can't tell anyone what we discuss." He pushed the bill back at me.

"Shawn, I am not your attorney now or ever," I said as loudly and clearly as I could. That much I wanted Micci to hear, or her answering machine to pick up.

I didn't want to get shot by this mad man. I'd stated that I wasn't his attorney and that would have to be enough.

He shook his head. "I paid you and so you are."

I didn't argue.

As if he'd solved things in his own mind he said, "How did you find out? I told Mom that she should drop things with you after we found out who you were. You had too much notoriety. Mom said that was why you'd be such a great mark. You wouldn't want to bring any more attention on yourself. She was wrong. I was right. But she never listened to me."

I still didn't say anything. I was digesting what he'd just said.

Mom.

Velma was Shawn's mother.

SP. Hawkins. Shawn P. Hawkins. He'd said Velma's son's name was Paul. Shawn Paul.

They were all the same.

I was thrilled that Micci was hearing this. "Where did Hawkins come from?"

"It's my last name. My father's name. Mom used to say it was the only good thing he ever left me. Do you know what it's like to have a father who leaves?"

I thought of my dad. We might have some distant times, but I never thought he'd leave me. "No."

"Or a mom who was certifiably crazy?" Shawn asked.

"I hardly remember my mother. I should remember more. I was young when she died, and I can't tell where my memory starts and where stories about her pick up. Things I remember because of pictures in the photo album that aren't real memories." I shook my head. "I miss her and yet I hardly remember her. That's weird, right?"

Shawn didn't say anything.

"What do you want, Shawn?" I asked.

"I'm leaving town. I just want you to stop looking into me. Stop hounding me. This isn't my fault. None of it is my fault. She made me do it all.

She never let me have friends. She pulled me out of school when I was fifteen."

"So you're not an attorney," I said. It was a statement, not a question.

"I could have been. I could have been anything. But no, she bought the RV when I was fifteen. We left home then and we've been moving ever since. We'd stay long enough to make a score, then we'd move somewhere else."

Flatter a kidnapper. Become real to them. I'd read that or heard that somewhere.

"That must have been hard," I said, commiserating.

If Micci was listening, I was pretty sure she'd be here soon. I hoped so at least.

If not, the answering machine had probably turned off.

Shawn said, "I tried to keep up with my schooling online. Velma always found Internet connections because it made scamming people easier if you could look things up on them. That connection meant I could study. And I did. She sneered and said all the books in the world wouldn't make me smart."

He was quiet a long time. I tried to think of something else to say to him, to reach him.

"I was smart enough to tell her to leave you alone after I figured out who you were. Would she listen? No. She made me call you. You'd caught a killer, you were a real lawyer, and she knew you suspected her of scamming you, but you couldn't prove it. Beating you made her happy. But when I didn't get the money and told

221

her I was sure you knew, she told me to try again. I said no. She hit me, over and over and over. I told her stop. I told her. But she wouldn't. She pulled the gun out of her purse. And then..."

"And then?" I prompted softly.

He glared at me. "You know. You've known from the beginning. You figured her out and you figured me out."

"So why are you here, Shawn?" I asked. "You can get in your RV and leave. You'd be free and clear."

"I'm so tired of running. I want to find a place and stay there. I want to find a...home." There was no anger in that proclamation. There was...longing.

Home...that was a universal desire. Everyone wanted somewhere to belong, even someone like Shawn.

"So how are you going to make that happen?" I asked softly.

"I'm going to ask you not to say anything. That's why I hired you. You can't talk to the police now that you're my attorney."

I shook my head. "Shawn, that's really not how attorney-client privilege works. I might not practice, but I'm still an attorney. I have to report crimes."

He sighed. "I know. I read enough to know that. But I just hoped..."

That gun. I needed to get that gun away from him. He'd shot someone once, I didn't want to be his next victim.

"Shawn, I have a friend. I could call her," I said slowly, trying to avoid looking at that gun.

"Another attorney?" he asked.

"I know one of those, too. But..." I hesitated a moment, hoping this was the right decision. "I was thinking about the detective who was investigating your mom."

"The one you were helping?" he asked, more agitated than before.

"She's a friend," I said quickly. "She helped out after my unfortunate incident."

That seemed to calm his anger. "The body in the kiln? That's what you're calling it?" He actually chuckled.

That laughter made me think maybe he wasn't going to shoot me. I forced a small smile as I said, "It sounds better than the body in my kiln."

The laughter died and Shawn said, "If you call your friend the detective, she'll arrest me."

"Probably. But it sounds as if there were extenuating circumstances," I said. "It sounds as if you didn't have a choice. Self-defense."

"I told Mom no. No more scams. No more moving. I'd get a job and support us. She laughed and said what kind of job could a high school dropout get?"

"Let me call Micci." I used her first name, thinking that made her seem less ominous than detective. "She understands that sometimes things just happen."

"She hit me and hit me and then Mom pulled the gun on me. She pulled it out of her purse. She pulled it out and said she wished I'd never been born. She said that I ruined her life. On and on. Then she said she could right that wrong. She could get rid of me now."

He was crying. "And then all the years of taking her guff. All the years of being her servant. All the years of never living my life, just serving hers hit me. She raised the gun and..." He paused and then whispered, "I hit her. She dropped the gun and I picked it up and pointed it at her. *Shoot me*, she said. *Show me you're a man and shoot me.* When I didn't, she started laughing and saying over and over, 'I knew you couldn't do it.' Then she grabbed at my hand as if she were going to take the gun away from me and...it just went off."

"Shawn, it sounds like there were extenuating circumstances. Let me call Micci. She'll help."

"No one can help me now. No one. My life's over and it never really got started." He picked the gun off his lap and lifted it. I wasn't sure if he was going to shoot me or himself, but I wasn't going to take a chance. I ducked under a table, ready to crawl to the door.

Then I heard a clatter. He threw the gun on the floor. I could see where it landed.

"Make your call, Harry," he said.

I came out from under the table, hung up my phone. I wasn't sure how much Micci had caught, if any. I called her number again.

She picked right up.

224

"Micci. It's Harry. You're on speaker phone right now," I said as a warning. "Can you get over to my place right away?"

There was a hesitation on her end and she said, "I was just pulling in at your place. I wanted to talk about next month's classes. I'll be right in."

She hung up and I called Micah. "I know you're getting ready for your sister's visit, but could you come over please?"

"What's wrong?" he asked.

I could hear the panic in his voice. "I'm fine," I reassured him, "but I've got a new client for you."

"Honestly, Harry. What did you do now? Who's the client?"

"Velma's son," I said. I didn't want to try to explain the rest right now.

Micah obviously didn't need me to say more. His swearwords were of the more standard variety. There was more than one F-bomb.

"I'm fine, Micah," I said over and over again as he swore not at me but at the circumstance.

"I was on my way over because I missed you. *Don't. Do. Anything.*"

I hung up and looked at Shawn, who hadn't said anything or moved. "There. I've called the detective and an attorney for you."

"Why would you help me?" Shawn asked.

"Listen, I have a father who is wonderful, but who had very clear ideas of who he wanted

225

me to be and what he wanted me to do with my life. It took a divorce to show me that this was my life and I deserve to be happy. I took control of my own happiness and here I am, an ex-attorney potter. You have a chance to take control of your life now."

"I killed my mother. How do you come back from that?" Shawn asked.

I didn't want to say that Velma wasn't much of a mother. I didn't know much about parenting, but I did know that a real parent wants their kids to be happy. Even when my father pushed me towards the law, it wasn't some maleficent plan on his behalf. He loved the law and thought I would too. The fact I didn't would always be a mystery to him.

"It was an accident. And frankly, she tried to shoot you. It was self-defense. Micah will help you. He's the best."

At the moment, I heard footsteps on the stairs. Since Micci didn't have a key, I knew it was Micah.

He threw open the door and pulled me into his arms. "Damn it, Harry, you've got to stop this."

"I swear, I didn't—"

I didn't finish the sentence because he was kissing me. At which point, he seemed to remember we had a murderer in the room. He turned to Shawn.

Micci was in the room too. She must have followed Micah up.

"This is Shawn Hawkins," I said to Micah. "Micci, you already know him as Velma's attorney. But he's more than that, he's Velma's son. He killed her, but it was self-defense. More of an accident than anything."

I realized Micci's gun was drawn. "It's okay, Micci. Shawn's gun's over there."

She picked it up, emptied the bullets and bagged it all up.

"Why is Micah here?" she asked, eyeing me with suspicion. "And how did he get here so fast."

"I was coming over regardless, but now I'm here because I'm representing Mr. Hawkins," Micah said.

Micci glared at me, then at Micah. "Of course you are. Okay, let's take this all down to the station. Mr. Hawkins, I need to cuff you."

Micah nodded at Shawn. "It's okay. She's going to take you down to the station and Harry and I will be right behind you. Don't say anything to anyone until I'm with you."

Shawn nodded.

Micah turned to Micci. "We'll be right behind you."

She nodded. "I'll need your statement, Harry."

"I know." I hated that I knew. I mean, as an attorney, I knew stuff like that, but I shouldn't know it on a personal basis.

"We'll follow you to the station," Micah said.

Micci and Shawn left. Micah didn't say anything as I let Lily out of the bedroom and gave her a huge dog bone as a treat.

"She tried to protect me," I said.

Micah leaned down and patted her head. "Good girl," he said, then looked up at me and said, "We've got to go."

"I know. I swear, I didn't do anything this time. I talked to a few friends and gave the information to Micci. This one wasn't me."

"I know," he said.

"My dad's going to be upset. And Phyllis will be too I imagine. I mean, I always wanted a mother, but not so I could torture one more person. I didn't ask for any of this. The *unfortunate incident* and now this."

"Will you be naming this one, too?" He shot me a look, telling me that he was as concerned as I was, but he understood this wasn't my fault and thought some humor would help.

I played along. "*Unfortunate Incident Part Two?*"

He shook his head. "That's a mouthful."

"*Slip and Fall?*"

"Better." He took my hand. "Grab your coat. We really have to go."

I felt like an old pro minutes later when we walked into the police department. I was sure I'd seen the woman behind the desk before. "Detective Dana—"

She interrupted me. "Is expecting you. I know. Harry, since I see you so often, I should probably introduce myself. I'm Tamara."

"Thanks, Tamara. Hopefully this is the last time you'll see me for a while." Seriously, two incidents in one lifetime—in two months—was too much.

"Forever," Micah corrected. "Not for a while."

I nodded my agreement.

Tamara buzzed us back and said, "The detective said wait in the interview room."

I didn't need to ask for directions. I knew the way. "Thank you."

"Any time," she said as she shot me a sympathetic look.

"Never again," Micah muttered as we made our way down the hall.

"I agree. I'm done. Even if a dead body drops from the sky and lands at my feet, I'm just turning around and walking away."

"Seriously. Don't walk, run," Micah said.

I kissed his cheek. "Promise. I'll run and never even ask why there was a dead body flying through the sky."

Micci came into the room to take my statement. Before she turned on the recorder, she stage-whispered, "Nice idea calling my cell."

Then she turned all business and took my statement.

After she clicked off the recorder she said, "Stay here while I take Micah next door and question Shawn.

"I won't move a muscle," I promised.

They both looked skeptical.

Tamara came back with a cup of coffee. "I figured you could use this."

"Thanks. I can. I'm normally an early-to-bed, early-to-rise sort. Late nights kill me."

I realized what I said and took a fortifying sip of the worst coffee I'd ever tasted. I mean, *worst*. It was as if gasoline and Brussel sprouts had a baby.

Yeah, I hate Brussel sprouts.

My face must have reflected my disgust because Tamara nodded sympathetically. "I know. It's bad. It's always bad. I make a nice cup of coffee at home, but even when I make it here, it comes out tasting like that. I think the coffee machine is cursed."

"I believe it." I didn't want to offend her, so I pretended to take another sip and then put the coffee cup on the table. I'd power through my sleep deprivation uncaffeinated.

"I came to your shop a few weeks ago," Tamara said. "I bought three of your Santas. I was only going to buy two. One for my mom and one for my mother-in-law, but they were so cute, I bought one for myself as well. I suspect it's going to be my favorite Christmas present this year. Last year my husband got me socks. Very nice socks, but seriously, socks."

I laughed and despite how bad the coffee was, I picked it up and took another sip. "I hope you come back to the shop soon. I've got these rabbits I'm doing for Easter that are one of my favorite new designs."

She grinned. "You can bet I will. I was coming in for one of those Bee mugs. My friend Mary Lee has a birthday after the new year. I want to do something special for her."

"If you call ahead, I can personalize something for her," I said.

"That would be awesome." She bubbled away for a few more seconds as I took a sip of the awful coffee, then hurried out when someone called her name.

I was alone in the interrogation room again. My thoughts went round and round as I tried to decide how I found myself in this position again. I lived a quiet life. I worked at a job I loved. Hung out with friends and I had a growing family. I'd met a man I really cared for. Maybe even more than that.

It should be an amazing time in my life.

And yet, here I was at the police department...again. I'd been held at gunpoint. I'd solved another murder...well, solve-ished.

I knew that something was up with Shawn Esquire. The truth was, he'd never even finished high school. And though his contract was off, it was very good for someone without a high school, college diploma, or law degree.

For years, I'd blamed my father for not supporting my dreams of art, but he had simply wanted me to find a career that was safe and could support me. And when push came to shove, he'd been behind me every step of the way. He loved me. No matter what had happened in our lives, I never doubted that he loved me.

At some point I must have laid my head down, because next thing I knew, Micah was giving me a little shake. "Come, sweetheart. I'm taking you home."

"Good. Lily's probably worried," I said.

He chuckled. "I doubt that dog woke up long enough to miss you."

"She did try to save me from Shawn," I said in defense of my dog.

"She gets an extra big dog bone for Christmas," he promised.

When we were settled in the car, I asked, "How's Shawn?"

"He's going to do some time, but it sounds like having Velma as a mother was pretty much a life sentence. We'll need to see if the ballistics report matches his story, but I think it will."

"She was an awful lady," I said.

"She was. But that's not why I agreed to be his attorney. I'm helping him because you asked, but truth be told, I wanted to deck him for holding a gun on you."

"He didn't really hold it on me. He just—"

"Shh. I don't think I can talk about it anymore tonight. You could come spend the night at my house."

"Lily," I reminded him.

"Then I'm inviting myself to sleepover, and I'm planning to take you up on that offer and move a few things to your place soon."

"I'd like that," I said.

I liked everything about Micah McCain.

Chapter Twelve

"There's a beauty in my practical and non-assuming pieces like a bowl or cup. They're functional, but they can be art as well."
~Harry's Pottery

The next day, Micah went home to get ready for the wedding.

The apartment felt empty without him.

Lily and I took a long walk before I headed over to my father's.

I started blubbering moments after I walked into his house and saw him in a new suit.

My father was not a new-suit sort of guy.

He wore suits from decades ago because they were *perfectly-fine-Harry.*

Today's suit was tailored with modern sensibilities in mind. He looked as if he could be on the cover of GQ. His salt-and-pepper hair was perfectly combed. His smile was broad.

My father looked happy.

Totally, over-the-moon happy.

That's when I started to cry.

"Harriet?" he said, concern in his voice. "Harry?" he asked quietly, using the nickname he normally avoided.

I came prepared and dabbed at my eyes with a tissue. "You just look so happy."

"I am," he said.

That. That was what I'd always wanted for my father.

"Where's Phyllis?" I asked.

"She doesn't want me to see her until the ceremony, so she's in the bedroom." He looked up the stairs with so much longing in his eyes, I almost started crying again, but I held myself in check.

"Do you think she wants company?" I asked.

"I know she does. I want to thank you for last night and—"

I cut him off. "Dad, I adore her. I'm so happy for you both. And frankly, I'm happy for me and Dylan, too. We get a family expansion."

"Did I hear my name?" Dylan asked as he walked in.

"You did, *little brother*. I said I was happy I was going to be your big sister. I never had a younger sibling to torture and I'm looking forward to honing my skills."

"Harriet does like to be the best at whatever she does. Law. Pottery. Siblings," my father, my serious father, said teasing as if he'd done it all his life. He turned to me. "I'm sure you'll excel."

"Thanks, Dad. I'm going to leave you boys alone and go check on Phyllis."

I didn't mention last night. That could wait. Today should only be about happy news.

Speaking of happy, I hadn't seen Micah yet, but I knew he'd be here.

I went up the stairs and knocked on my father's bedroom door. "Phyllis, it's Harry."

"Come in, dear."

I opened the door and started crying again. Phyllis was wearing an ivory skirt and jacket with the slightest lace overlay. She had on a string of pearls and matching earrings.

"As your maid of honor, I brought you something to borrow. It's old and blue." I reached in my pocket—yes, the dress had a pocket which made it the most awesome dress in the history of dresses—and pulled out my grandmother's sapphire ring. "It was Dad's mother's. He gave it to me for my eighteenth birthday, which was how old my grandmother was when she got married. I thought you might like to wear it today, sort of a connection to his past. A sign that you're part of the family."

"Oh, Harry," she said as she slipped it on her finger and started to cry.

I felt my eyes start to leak. "Phyllis, don't. We can't cry. We both look awesome and don't want to mess up our makeup and..."

We both cried and hugged each other and touched up our makeup when we were done.

"I look okay?" she asked.

"You look beautiful," I assured her.

Almost on cue, there was a knock on the door. "Mom, it's time."

We walked out and I led the way down the stairs. There was no music to set a pace to, but I walked slower than I normally would.

And as we turned the corner, I saw Micah. He had on a super slim-cut, black suit and a very fashionable dark blue tie that complimented the blue blush to my pocketed dress. He pushed his glasses up higher on his nose and I felt all swoony.

I turned around and Phyllis looked as if she felt swoony, too.

One of Dad's friends stood in front of the Christmas tree. "Normally, I'd start with dearly beloved, but today, Phyllis and Josiah have a different idea."

My dad turned to Phyllis. "Phyllis, You came to the office and put things to right...things I hadn't even realized needed fixed. And slowly, I realized that more than just my office needed fixed. I did. You reminded me to be a father, not my daughter's boss, or ex-boss as the case may be. You reminded me to take time off and enjoy myself from time to time. You reminded me what it feels like to be half of a whole. Today's just a formality. You've been my other half since the morning you told me that if I barked at you for coffee one more time I'd be wearing it. That was the moment I realized that I was in love with you and had been in love long before that."

He kissed her.

"Josiah, I refuse to comment on the fact that you fell in love with me when I threatened you. I knew I loved you that day. I'd known for a long time. I wasn't sure how you felt, or if you'd ever really notice me. And finally, I took matters into my own hands. And here we are. Everyone seemed surprised that we'd planned such a small affair, but Josiah, you gave me everything I wanted today...you gave me your love and yourself. Nothing else matters. I love you."

She kissed him.

When my father placed the ring on Phyllis's finger, he saw my grandmother's ring and glanced at me. I nodded and he smiled at me.

The judge pronounced them husband and wife and the champagne was served and the cake was cut.

Micah was suddenly at my side. "Harry, you took my breath away when you stepped into the room."

"You took mine away as well. I—"

I was going to say those three words. I could taste them on my tongue. But Dylan was calling my name. "Speech. Speech."

For a moment, I froze. I'm not sure if it was almost saying *I love you* to Micah or the fact I had to make an impromptu speech.

I took a deep breath and said, "Growing up, it was just me and my father. He really tried to be mother and father to me, even when talking about girl things made him uncomfortable. He just muddled through it. He always tried to give me everything I needed and most of what I wanted.

"But as much as my father and I were a complete, I used to dream about a larger family. Siblings. A mom. It might have taken a little longer than I'd hoped, but today he's given me a brother and a mother. I know our lives will never be the same...they'll be better because of it. So welcome to the family, Phyllis and Dylan."

I raised my glass and everyone toasted.

Dylan said, "I knew a speech was beyond me, so I'll just point to my new big sister and say, *What she said.*" He raised his glass and everyone toasted again.

Dad's house wasn't huge, but there was plenty of room for the twenty or so people to fan out. I was sitting on the stairs when Micah came over with a second piece of cake. "I thought you might help me with this. If I eat it myself, I'm a pig, but if you help me eat it, I'm romantic."

He handed me a fork.

It was a delicious cake, so I was happy to oblige.

"I didn't mention last night to your father or Phyllis," he said.

"Me either. They deserve one day to be totally happy. I don't want them worrying about me. Especially since it all came out okay in the end."

"But Harry, it could have ended differently. I'll have nightmares about that for some time to come. You know, I started to say earlier that you took my breath away when you walked in the room. I know we haven't known each other a long time, but I want to tell you that I—"

"Harry," Dylan called. "Mom wants you. She's throwing the bouquet."

I hurried out, Micah's words left unspoken. Maybe it was better. We'd only known each other such a short time and...

"Harry," Phyllis said. "Catch..." She threw the bouquet at me with no fuss or ceremony.

"You're the only single girl here, so you win by default."

"I'm not sure having the threat of marriage hanging over my head is a win," I grumbled.

Phyllis shot my father a besotted look. "It is. It really is."

That.

All this romance and craziness is why those three words were on my mind. I'd caught wedding-itis. As soon as I left, things would calm down.

I looked back at Micah.

"I think it's time for you two to get on the road. I'll clean up the house and close up," I said.

"Thank you dear. And what you said today...well, it means the world to me," Phyllis said.

"I'm so happy for you and Dad and for me and Dylan too, Phyllis."

They left, then the guests did as well.

Dylan stayed to help clean up. And then he left. Micah said, "Want to head down to *Down By the Bay* for dinner?"

"I do," I said. Those two words had me thinking about three words again.

We ate dinner and I studiously avoided our earlier conversation. Micah tried to turn the conversation in that direction but I changed it to the previous night. "What do you think will happen to Shawn?"

"I don't know, but if the evidence lines up with his story, I think I can get the DA to go for a deal."

"I feel sorry for him," I admitted. "I mean, what he did was horrible, but what his mother did to him was horrible as well. It doesn't justify her death, but..." I shrugged. "I'm not sure what I'm saying other than the whole situation stinks."

"You were so brave last night."

I snorted. "I was terrified."

"But you kept your head and, Harry—"

He looked serious and I worried about where the conversation was heading, so I said, "So Millie will be here in the morning."

He sighed. I was pretty sure he knew what I was doing. "Yes. You'll get to meet her.

"I can't wait."

I'll confess, I was nervous about meeting his sister. Or maybe I was simply nervous about what he'd started to say at my father's.

"Bring Lily. Millie loves dogs."

I laughed. "I just realized my dog's name rhymes with your sister's. She might not appreciate that."

"She won't mind."

After dinner, we walked Lily and I thought about asking Micah to come upstairs, but he said, "I'd invite myself up, but I need to get ready for Millie's visit. Rain check?"

"Rain check," I said.

And in case I misunderstood the fact he was leaving, he kissed long and longingly. "You'll be there for brunch?"

I nodded. "Yes. It feels weird not to do brunch at Dad's."

I hoped my father and Phyllis were having a great time. They weren't going on a traditional honeymoon. Rather they were driving down to southeastern PA and going to Koziar's Christmas Village. Phyllis had mentioned how much she loved it when she went as a kid. My father found a B&B nearby and planned a perfect couple day getaway.

"They're excited about Christmas dinner. I'm invited," he said as if checking with me. Sunday brunches were one thing, but holiday meals were something else entirely. We both understood that.

I nodded. "I'm glad."

"Millie's leaving on a plane Christmas Eve. Her cruise leaves Christmas morning." He paused a moment. "She normally wouldn't even visit near Christmas. She hates the holiday. Seriously hates it. She likes to travel and ignore the season as much as the decorations will allow."

I wasn't sure what I'd make of his Scrooge sister, but planned to try to like her for Micah's sake.

He kissed me "Throw the deadbolt," he said.

"I will. And I'll see you tomorrow."

He was right. Lily didn't even lift her head when I climbed in bed.

I worried I'd have nightmares.

But I didn't.

Instead I dreamed of Micah.

That wasn't a nightmare by any stretch of the imagination.

I'd planned on wearing the cute Christmas tree earrings I'd made, but opted not, given Millie's rumored Scrooge-ish nature.

I wanted her to like me, and I felt a bit pathetic about that.

It was storming when I woke up. I mean a full-on lake effect storm.

The snow whipped at my window. It was a hard snow, not the light fluffy stuff. It made tink, tink, tink sounds as it hit the glass.

This was the kind of day I'd normally enjoy the fact that I worked and lived in the same location. On days like this, I reveled in the fact my morning commute was a walk down the backstairs.

Even Lily took a look outside and balked at the idea of going out. I physically gave her a nudge out the door and she hurried out to take care of her morning business.

She gave me an *I-don't-envy-you* look as I bundled up to go to Micah's. And despite his invitation, I took pity on her and left her behind.

I drove at a snail's pace. But I made it in one piece and knocked on the door knowing the butterflies in my stomach were no longer about the ride to Micah's but rather about meeting his sister.

His sister was the one who opened the door.

"You must be Harry. I'm Millie, though I bet you already deduced that. Rumor has it you're rather Sherlocky."

I stepped inside and made sure to stand on the mat because I was shedding snow at an alarming rate as I took off my coat and hat. I slipped off my boots and left them there.

"I am Harry and it's nice to meet you, Millie. I've heard a lot about you." Now that wasn't really a lie. Micah had told me he had parents, a sister and grandparents who met every year at a camp for a family reunion-ish celebration. I knew that Millie was a great lover of baths and smelly stuff. And I knew she didn't celebrate Christmas.

"I saw that small tree you gave Micah. Our family doesn't do trees normally, I mean, the whole Jewish thing and all," she said bluntly.

"You're Jewish?"

"He didn't tell you?" She sighed. "We're not really. We're Irish Catholic and Jewish. We avoid picking a religious holiday by not celebrating any. I was impressed Micah broke with the family tradition. I think I travel during the holidays so that I can enjoy all the decorations without feeling guilty about it."

"That is not exactly how your brother explained things," I said slowly. I didn't want to throw Micah under the holiday bus, but maybe he deserved it just a bit. I'd been worried about

Millie because of the way he'd framed what he'd told me about her.

"Aw, he painted me as a Grinch?" Millie asked.

And while I wasn't about to throw him under the bus, but I wasn't going to let him off the hook either. We would be talking about this later.

She nodded when I didn't say anything, neither confirming nor denying her supposition. "Micah's cooking, so why don't we go sit in front of the tree and visit."

She led me to the living room and that tree I'd given him, unwittingly breaking his family tradition.

"You made all the ornaments?" she asked.

I nodded.

"You really are very talented," she said.

"Thanks. I feel lucky to be working at something I love for a living," I said. It hit me all over again just how very lucky I was.

"Loving your vocation is a blessing," Millie said. "And what about this new avocation?"

"Pardon?"

"Your amateur sleuthing?"

"I'm not..." I shook my head. "I'm leaving the designation *Erie's Amateur Sleuth* to Quincy Mac. I just had a couple unfortunate incidents. That's not an avocation, that's just bad luck."

"Did Micah mention what I do for a living?" she asked.

I shook my head. "It seems there's a lot Micah didn't mention."

I knew that wasn't fair. I felt so comfortable with him that it was hard to remember I'd only known him since November. Not even quite two months. I was hoping we had a long time to get to know all the stories about each other. I hadn't told him much about my ex. And I know I'd never told him about my mother.

Yeah, it was tough to be annoyed.

"I thought I heard you come in," Micah said as he poked his head in the room. "Brunch will be on the table in a few minutes."

"Do you need help?" I asked, hoping he'd say yes so I could kiss him, because at the moment, I had a very real urge to do just that.

"No, I've got it. You two just get to know each other."

Millie studied me a moment with the intensity of a scientist looking at a specimen. "Wow, you have it as bad as he does."

"Have *it?*"

She didn't answer, though I guess she didn't need to. I did have *it* bad. Maybe it hadn't been two months, but Micah had woven himself into the fabric of my life.

"Before we go sit down and eat and you two googly eye each other through the meal, I want to get back to what I do for a living."

I cocked my head, waiting.

"I'm a reporter. And I think there's a story in your recent series of..." She paused. "What did you call them?"

I sighed. *"Unfortunate incidents."*

She laughed. "Right. I know there was a few short national stories after the kiln, and I suspect there will be more now."

"I didn't solve anything technically," I pointed out.

"Still, a private eye potter is a great hook. And Micah says you're writing a book. This would be great promotion."

"I'm not writing a book of fiction. It's a book about pottery. It's got a specific, limited audience," I said.

"That's a mistake. Why not cast a broader net? Sure write about pottery. Write about the art of it. But write something that's a bit more memoir-y. Something like *Harry's Pottery...The Art of the Journey*. Something about finding your passion and going for it. That would have a much broader appeal. Or *Harry's Pottery...A Memoir, A Pottery How-To and Amateur Sleuth Story*. Okay, that sucks, but you get the picture. As a reporter, I want to reach the broadest audience I can. Writing about a woman who literally has people dropping like flies around her...that's a story."

It might seem like just a story to her—a hooky story even—but it was my life. I wasn't sure how comfortable I was capitalizing on tragedy. "I'll think about it."

"Food's on," Micah called.

He had impeccable timing. "Coming," I called.

Millie said, "I really hope you'll think about it, Harry. I can almost guarantee reporters will be sniffing around this story. If you let me tell it, you're guaranteed to have a friend behind the pen."

She reached in her pocket and pulled out a card. "I'll be back from my cruise New Year's Day. I'd like to talk then."

"We can talk, but truly, I'm just hoping this all gets swept away in the new year. I feel more like a confession magnet than an amateur sleuth."

I was going to have to confess everything to my dad when he got home. That was all the confessing I planned on doing.

Millie nodded and said, "My advice on the book is solid. You're looking to cast a wide net for readers. I read this book, *Victuals: An Appalachian Journey*, with recipes. It was by this author, Ronni Lundy. It was at its heart a cookbook with a side dose of travel guide and a bit of memoir. It was a fascinating read. And I don't cook—Micah inherited those genes. But it almost made me wish I *did* cook."

"You have never wished you could cook a day in your life," Micah said as he came out with one more plate from the kitchen.

"We were talking about a book and it did make me wish I could cook. Of course, as I read the book, I got take-out."

"Millie's greatest skill is ordering food," he teased.

"Everyone has to have a skill set," she quipped back.

"Did she harangue you?" Micah asked me.

"She had some very good advice for the book," I said.

He looked at his sister, obviously not quite believing me.

"Really, she did," I insisted.

He shrugged. "I guess there is a first time for everything."

"I take umbrage with that comment," Millie said. "And I now seek revenge by relaying an embarrassing story from your past, *Tennyson*."

She said the name of the poet with a great deal of emphasis. I didn't need to be a reporter to know there was a story there.

"Millie," Micah said, warning in his voice.

She stood, cleared her voice and clasped her hands in front of her.

"The girl I like is sweet.
"She's happy all the time.
"She makes me stuff to eat.
"I'm awfully glad she's mine.
"I took her to the movies.
"She let me hold her hand.
"She's a cheerleader for the team.
"And I play drums in the band.
"I—"

"Millicent McCain, if you say one more word—one—I'm going to call Mom and Dad and tell them about Bart," Micah said.

She unclasped her hands and sat down quickly. "You wouldn't."

"I would. If I were going to Tennyson today I'd say something about *I like a girl named*

Harry and letting my sister meet her is scary so Millie better be bewarey or I'll tell Mom and Dad she's married."

Honestly, all the color drained from Millie's face and I could see that Micah realized he went to far. "Mill, I wouldn't. I mean—"

"Micah, there are things we can tease each other about. Your bad poetry and my cooking...both are fair game. But that—I'll borrow Harry's term—that *unfortunate incident* will never be teasing fodder."

"Got it. Sorry." He paused a moment and said, "I'm really sorry."

She nodded and he looked relieved.

I grabbed at some other talking point. "So where are you cruising too?"

"No idea. Islands. I mainly just want to get out of town so coworkers aren't inviting me to parties or asking what my family's doing for the holiday. It gets awkward trying to explain our non-holiday-philosophy."

Whatever the Bart thing was, it had blown over. And as the day went on, I realized I liked Micah's sister. I helped with dishes, then bowed out, leaving the siblings an evening together.

As I was saying my goodbyes, Millie asked, "I'll call you after the new year?"

It was a question or maybe a threat. But I smiled and said, "Sure. Have a great trip."

Micah walked me to the door. "Don't let Millie bully you. When she gets an idea, she's like a dog with a bone."

"She gave me some good advice," I said.

He gave me a questioning look.

"She did. About the book," I assured him.

He nodded and that was that. I kissed him and left him to visit with his sister.

I got home then took Lily out for a walk.

It was cold. The frigid Canadian air blew across the lake and bit any exposed skin. I was too caught up in my thoughts to really mind. They went round and round.

Millie's advice on the book.

Her request for an interview.

Another murderer in custody.

Someone else in my orbit murdered.

Another holiday season under my belt.

A new year on its way.

New classes at the shop.

A new relationship.

My father's new marriage.

A new stepbrother.

I didn't follow through any thought very long. I'd try to concentrate on the book, then thoughts of my father would insert themselves. So I'd think about how happy he was with his new relationship. That would remind me how happy I was with Micah and…

Round and round.

"Harry?"

I stopped in the middle of the west side of Perry Square. "Micci?"

She gave me a look that made me realize she must have been calling my name more than once. "Sorry. I was thinking."

"You weren't just thinking, you were lost in thought," she corrected me. "I saw you walking through the park and thought I'd save myself a trip to your place."

"Oh, come on. I'm getting hauled in for questioning again?"

Honest to Pete, this was getting old real fast.

She laughed. "No. I'm saying thank you. Thanks for all your help and for trying to stay out of things. Shawn's confessed to everything."

"So it's over?" I asked.

"It's over."

I sighed. "Good. I'm done with dead bodies. I hereby proclaim next year is a dead body free year."

"I second that goal," Micci said with a laugh. "The only time I want to see you next year is when I take that class."

I held out my hand and shook hers. "Deal."

"Merry Christmas, Harry."

"Merry Christmas, Micci."

Lily and I walked through the Christmas light lit park after Micci headed back across the street and into the police station.

My thoughts might be tumbling over themselves but one thing I was certain about...no more dead bodies.

Epilogue

"Disney says it's the 'Happiest Place on Earth.' Since this is a book about pottery I should probably say that my happiest place is behind a pottery wheel. But it's not. My happiest place is with the people I love...and then in my studio."
~Harry's Pottery

On Christmas morning, we all sat around opening our gifts. I was pleased when Phyllis opened her mug. It read *Smom*.

"Smom?" she asked as she ran her hand over the words I'd printed in it.

"Well, Mom is already taken and calling you by your first name seems disrespectful. Stepmom is too cumbersome and no one actually calls their stepmother's that. So I landed on Smom. Short for stepmom, but close to mom. I haven't had a mother in so long...having one now is my best Christmas gift."

Phyllis burst into tears and hurried across the room to hug me. I hugged her back. I suspect it was a bit awkward. Dad and I weren't huggy sorts of people. But Phyllis didn't seem to mind.

Then Dylan and I gave her the handprints we'd made. I wanted it to look like those handprints young kids made for their parents. I wrote our names under them.

Phyllis cried all over again.

The day was perfect.

Dylan smiled when he opened his rainbow mug embossed with his name.

Dad hefted his and said, "I will never not have a Harry mug for my coffee. Thanks, honey."

I waited to exchange gifts with Micah until we were back at my place. I felt nervous as he unwrapped his mug. I'd rushed to get it done in my small test kiln. He studied it for what seemed eternity. I'd written, *'Love is the only gold.' ~Tennyson"*

"So you've joined with my sister to mock me," he said with a grin.

"Maybe at first. I found a Tennyson quote, *'Hope smiles from the threshold of the year to come, whispering, 'It will be happier.'* I was going to use that. I'd almost used the L word so many times. I stopped myself every time because I told myself logically it was too soon. But that seemed cowardly. I'm not expecting you to say them back, but for Christmas I wanted to say them. I love you."

There.

I'd said the words.

I waited for him to at least say *thank you.* Or *you're right, it is too soon.* But instead, he scooped me off the couch as if I weighed next to nothing, put me on his lap and said, "For the record, I love you, too."

The rest of our gifts were forgotten as we lost ourselves in the greatest Christmas gift...love.

Award-winning author Holly Jacobs has over three million books in print worldwide. The first novel in her Everything But... series, Everything But a Groom, was named one of 2008's Best Romances by Booklist, and her books have been honored with many other accolades. She lives in Erie, Pennsylvania, with her family. You can visit her at www.HollyJacobs.com